COUNTRY GOLD

HEATHERLY BELL

HEATHERLY BELL BOOKS

Dear Reader,

Reunion romances are my favorites. Lexi and Luke have been apart for a year due mostly to circumstances beyond their control. When he returns to his hometown of Whistle Cove, Luke has a bit of groveling to do. He's been lured by fame and temporarily lost sight of what's important. But now that he's decided to put his life back together, it may be too late.

At the heart of this book is the pressure of public perception and image and how it can affect personal relationships. Imagine living your life when everyone is watching your every move. This is what Luke has to deal with when he quickly shoots up to stardom and loses touch with the small things that matter in life.

Thank you for coming along with me on this new adventure into the world of Whistle Cove. Although the small town is completely fictional, the central coast setting is very real. Monterey Bay is one of the most beautiful areas in the country.

I'm fortunate to live within drivable distance. Years ago, as a young adult new to California, I fell in love with the area. I have many fond memories of 17-mile drive and trips to the beach, both with friends, and later with my own family.

You will find the mention of real locations, including the Monterey Bay Aquarium, Cannery Row, the Wharf, and The Crow's Nest (which is actually in neighboring Santa Cruz.) However, some of the places are plucked from my own vivid imagination, so you will not find the Wilder Sisters B&B, or Lulu's Day Spa. The lavish beauty of this area is sometimes hard to get across in simple words, and I hope I've done it justice.

If you're ever in central California, you must drop by Monterey Bay and tell me what you think. I love to hear from you.

With deep regard,

~ Heatherly

CHAPTER 1

Behind every little sister there's a big sister standing, holding a bat, asking, "You want to say that again?" ~ Meme

The stage lights were blinding and for a moment Luke Wyatt thought he was seeing things. He blinked. Twice. No, *she* wasn't in the front row.

She hadn't been for a year, so why should tonight be any different?

The concert hall was packed as he ended with a reprisal of his #1 Billboard, chart-topping, cross-over country hit: *Falling for Forever*. After more than a year of playing it in a 90-city tour across the United States, he was frankly sick of the song. But the fans here in...crap, where the hell was he again? Austin? Yeah, Austin, Texas. Anyway, the fans everywhere loved it, so out it came as an encore.

Every.
Single.
Night.
A love song.
Joke was on him.

Despite the twelve *other* songs he'd also written, the one he'd penned with Lexi Wilder remained the fan favorite. His cash cow, everyone on his team said. His *ticket.*

"Good show." The road manager clapped Luke's back as he walked off the stage and handed the Gibson to his trusted roadie.

Luke guessed the show was about as good as it could be, considering he'd been on auto-pilot for the last leg of the tour. Dialing it in. He wondered how everyone had missed this. Along with the rest of his band, Luke was herded out the back door of the concert hall and straight to the tour bus parked at the curb waiting. Fans were gathered behind a barricade and loud claps and cheers rose as he and his band members emerged. Luke waved and went along the line, shaking hands, and taking selfies with as many fans as feasible. Moving quickly. He wished he could personally thank each and every one of his fans for buying his music instead of pirating it. For coming out to see the show instead of staying home with Netflix.

He boarded the tour bus, fist bumping with their driver and getting his phone back. Like the rest of the band, he never took his cell with him onstage since at worst it might ring or buzz during a quiet moment. At best it was a complete distraction. He moved towards the back as the rest of the band followed suit and filed in. It was the last night of their brutal tour opening for *Lady Antebellum.* The rest of his road crew would slowly trickle in and tonight they'd all be on their way back to Nashville. Maybe he'd actually get to spend some time there. Buy a house. He could afford to now, even if he wasn't too excited about the idea.

Gary, his manager, practically tackled Luke. It took everything in him not to groan in pain. He'd pushed himself too hard for the past year and his back was killing him from an old injury. Not that he would let anyone know that. Instead, he grimaced and hoped it might look like a grin.

"Great show!" Gary said.

"Thought I asked you not to blow smoke up my ass." Luke took a seat near the back.

Damn it all. He couldn't help his foul mood. It wasn't just the back pain, but he'd been on the road so long he hardly felt human. Sleeping during the day like a vampire. Sharing close quarters with a bunch of smelly dudes. Moving from one city to another and having no idea half the time *where* he was. Still, he recognized bullshit when he heard it. He wished the people around him would stop shoveling it.

"What's up? Weren't you happy with the set tonight?" Gary asked.

"Sure."

"The crowd loved it."

"Yeah." He'd remembered the words and played every lick on his guitar.

He liked to think it meant he wasn't that bad off.

But he missed the days when Gary would give him the unvarnished and painful truth. *It wasn't your best. Try that song in another key.* Now that he was a huge success, everyone was afraid to give him the slightest bit of honest criticism. Everyone but Lexi, that is, and he hadn't seen her in one long year.

He'd certainly never forget her despite what she believed. A man didn't forget the first slam to his heart. One look at her, and he'd been lost.

Lexi and her two younger sisters had been a squeaky clean, highly successful, CMA award-winning band for years. His first break came roading for them and later being part of their back-up band. Seeing the country from a tour bus. Getting, for once in his life, the best of everything.

Falling in love.

And then the sex scandal had happened.

Not involving Lexi, but her youngest sister, Sabrina. Private nude photos she'd texted to a guy she'd flirted with at a record label party had been sold to a tabloid magazine. Having spent her teenage years on a tour bus with her sisters, Sabrina was naïve about men, and she'd trusted the wrong person.

Though their devoted fans stood by them, record sales plummeted, and the girls were dropped. The label sought to salvage something out of the ashes and pushed him front and center. Lexi had written most of the Wilder Sister songs, so she co-wrote a single with him for the debut album. That album went gold within a month. Safe to say Luke Wyatt had come a long way from his humble beginnings as the son of the town murderer. All thanks to one Lexi Wilder, who years before had convinced her daddy (their manager at the time) to let him roadie for her band.

"Next stop, Nashville!" The driver called out when the last of the road crew had boarded.

"Home, baby!" James, the drummer, shouted.

"I wonder if my kids remember what I look like," said their bass player, Tom.

"Hell, I'm hoping my wife remembers me!" Gary said.

He clapped a hand on Luke's shoulder. "Hey, look, I can see you're tired but in Nashville you'll finally be able to kick off your boots, relax, and write us all some more hit songs."

Us. That was the problem. Since he'd written a #1 hit song with Lexi, offers were lining up to write with others. But he'd always been more of a lone wolf. That song with Lexi had been a fluke. A little bit of magic he'd love to repeat with her.

Any time. Any place.

Problem was she hated him now.

"I don't have a place to stay."

He'd lived like a nomad, but his last known address was actually a ramshackle cottage in his hometown of Whistle Cove on California's central coast. That old place had been condemned, but still, it was home. Those stark memories, both painful and tender, rolled through him.

"That's cool. You'll stay with me until you can rent or buy a place."

"No, I can't do that to you and Claire."

"Are you kidding? Claire's your biggest fan. She's probably going to be bugging you all the time, wanting you to sing to her. Taking selfies and putting them on her Friendbook page."

Luke slid him a look, folding his arms across his chest. "That's exactly what I'm worried about."

"Okay, you're right. You can stay with my brother until you get a place. He hates country music, and if it wasn't for me he wouldn't even know who you are."

But the problem in Nashville, where he'd been lauded as the next big thing in country music, the next huge crossover success, was that important things were expected of him. Big things. Such as more country gold. His stomach tensed. If he didn't deliver something soon, he'd be a one-hit wonder.

No pressure.

There was only one place on earth where the expectation of him remained less than stellar last he'd checked. Nothing much had ever been anticipated from the son of Reggie Wyatt, unless it involved wearing an orange prison jumpsuit. He'd have some anonymity there. No one much liked to come around the son of a convicted murderer. And the residents of Whistle Cove would prefer that the rest of the world not know they were the birthplace of Reggie Wyatt.

Therefore, he had a sort of built-in privacy in Whistle Cove.

He knew exactly where he would stay. The *Wilder Sisters*

B&B. The family business started by Lexi's paternal grand-mother was struggling. He'd offered to help, of course, but been turned down repeatedly by Lexi. Lexi, who stopped taking his calls. If she really didn't want anything more to do with him, she'd have to say this to his face.

"This is your life now, Luke. Live it." Those were the last words she'd said to him.

The pain of those words slammed through him like he'd just heard them yesterday. A life without her? Hell no, he didn't want that life. He hadn't signed up for that. He and Lexi had unfinished business.

"I'm headed home, Gary."

"Exactly. Nashville."

"No. California. My hometown."

"Wouldn't that be dangerous?"

Great. Now Gary was worried about him, as if he couldn't take care of his own damn self like he always had. He'd grown up on the waterfront of Monterey Bay, and it was true that he had enemies in Whistle Cove. Some of Reggie's friends still worked the docks and they had no respect for Luke. As a man, he shouldn't have ratted on his father. Never mind that he'd done the right thing.

"Take me to the closest airport before you guys head home," Luke directed their driver.

There was dead silence in the wake of that, followed by a chorus of "what the hell" and "what's up now."

Gary simply stared at him. "You need to get back to Nashville and re-group. Write some songs, and then get back into the studio. We've got people chomping at the bit to write with you."

"Look, you said it yourself. I need to relax and write some hit songs. And I might as well do it in my hometown."

"Is that such a good idea? What about security?"

"Don't worry about all that."

"I'm your friend and your manager. Worrying is what I do for a living now."

"Reggie's goons don't scare me."

He needed more time so he could get Lexi to at least listen to him. Get her to understand that he'd never meant to choose his career over her. And now, finally, he had given her the time and space she'd clearly wanted from him.

Time to face the music, baby.

Looking resigned, Gary caved. "Great. If the only thing you can get out of her is another hit song, it will be well worth the trip."

Luke ignored that comment. He'd write his own hits from now on. What he wanted from Lexi had nothing to do with a song.

"Meet up with y'all next week."

Maybe he needed a little perspective. Going back to Whistle Cove might be just the thing to find some inspiration, too. The place he'd first met the now infamous Wilder sisters.

Lexi would likely be less than ecstatic to see him. Too bad. He had some things to clear up with her, and she *would* listen.

Luke was headed home to Whistle Cove.

CHAPTER 2

"When I say I won't tell anyone, my sister doesn't count."~ Meme

*L*exi Wilder took a deep breath of the salty bay air. It was late morning and breakfast and clean up accomplished, she'd changed the linens in one vacant room and folded a stack of clean bath towels. Now break time. The comforting and steady hum of Monterey Bay. The squawking sound of the seagulls as they foraged for scraps of food abandoned in the sand. A mug of coffee in her hands, she settled back on the blue Adirondack chair that sat on a patch of the Wilder B&B's private access beach and closed her eyes.

"Seriously?" Sabrina's voice came from behind, ending all hope of a quiet moment. "You're such a show-off. You folded the stack of towels, too? That was my job."

"Most people would just say 'thank you.' So, you're welcome."

Sabrina plopped down in the empty chair next to Lexi, phone in hand, ear buds around her neck as usual. "You're going to make Gram think I never *do* anything around here. "

Sisters. Can't live with them, can't kill them without doing twenty-five to life.

Then again, Sabrina had a lot of making up to do around here after The Scandal as Gram referred to it. More than a year later, she was still working to settle the account on the damage Gran claimed had been done to the Wilder name. Which was funny, considering it was almost as if Sabrina had simply lived up to the family name.

"There's never a lack of jobs to do around here."

Especially not now that their grandmother had injured her knee while playing golf. At least she claimed it was golfing, though Lexi worried it might have more to do with the Clint Eastwood lookalike with whom she'd recently been spending all her free time. Her mind refused to go there. Not to a place where her grandmother had more game than Lexi did. You just couldn't slow the seventy-eight-year-old down. Even so, the sisters had taken over the running of the *Wilder Sisters B&B* with the help of a skeleton crew.

Next to Lexi, Sabrina settled in on the chair, leaned her head back and plugged in her earbuds. Within two seconds, she was singing along to *Body like a Back Road.* "Oh man, I love that Sam Hunt."

Lexi snorted and kept her eyes closed. Try to find a man Sabrina *didn't* love. This was part of her problem.

"You know the song isn't really about driving the back roads, right?"

"Uh-huh." Lexi took another sip of the magic beans and tried to imagine her sister wasn't sitting next to her, yakking away and disturbing the peace.

"It's about sex," Sabrina continued. "And I sure as hell would have sex with Sam Hunt. Like in a heartbeat."

"Shh."

"Oh!" Sabrina cried out and took one of her ear buds out, offering it to Lexi. *Falling for Forever* by Luke Wyatt played.

9

Lexi pulled the ear bud out with a glare and handed it back to her clueless sister. She did *not* want to hear that song or anything else by Luke. It was getting to where she couldn't risk listening to the radio anymore. He was on the top ten of…everything.

"What? It's your song, too!" Sabrina pulled both ear buds out. "You should be proud of it. And Luke wouldn't be where he is today if not for us."

Don't remind her. But Lexi wasn't going to cry about it. She was all cried out. She couldn't even listen to her own song because when she and Luke had co-written *that song* she'd been deeply in love with the man. And him? Well, he'd fooled her because at the time she'd definitely believed she wasn't alone in that.

"I don't know why you wouldn't claim any of the back-stage passes he left for you. I mean, what's it been, a year now since he went on tour?" Sabrina said.

"He can have himself a nice life, as far as I'm concerned."

She'd tried to send that message to him loud and clear. Some things were just tough to forgive. He'd chosen fame over her. Besides, there were all the rumors of him and plenty of women. Those hurt the most. She knew how the rumor mill worked, but photos were tough to argue with (Sabrina should know) and there were plenty of those with Luke, beauties hanging all over him. The first photo she'd seen had like been a punch to the heart. By the third one, she was numb, her heart encased in a slab of ice.

Then there was the whole matter of the rest of his gold-selling album. Luke had written those songs by himself, incredibly personal songs about *their* relationship. Their break-up. She was pissed off that he'd used her that way.

Eight years ago, she'd first met Luke at one of their shows. Standing in the back. Alone. The town bad boy, since some swore he'd follow in his father's footsteps, and based on his actions at the time, he'd been headed in that direction. With a father in prison for murder, Luke had been adrift from the time he was eighteen. A Juvenile delinquent record for street racing. Driving with a suspended license. His first speeding ticket: exhibition of speed.

But she'd taken one look in his dark eyes and had seen the warmth shimmering underneath those long black lashes. Her entire body hummed when he'd noticed her and smiled. It was tingling and sparking like a live wire, all feelings she'd never experienced.

He'd had no one left, and he'd needed a job, so she convinced her father to let him roadie for their group. It turned out that Luke actually played guitar quite well, and eventually, he'd graduated to playing back up for them.

All that seemed…a lifetime ago.

"Hey, guys. What are you doing?" Jessie joined them now, bringing a tray of caramelized apple muffins from the B&B's morning's spread. "Swiped these. This morning Mr. Jackson said they tasted like an angel's wing had been dipped in caramel and then dusted in apple crumbs."

Lexi rolled her eyes. "Maybe he should start writing songs."

"Hey, maybe," Jessie said. "I'll tell him you said that."

Lexi dug in, tasting the delicious tart sweetness rolling over her tongue and wishing she could marry a muffin. She was quite sure they'd be very happy together.

Jessie snatched the last muffin just as Sabrina reached for it. "Jessie! I was going to eat that."

"I'm saving you. These have way too many calories and you need to go on a diet," Jessie said, gambling with life and limb.

"You take that back!" Sabrina jumped out of her seat and was after Jessie, who ran away laughing.

Those two were only a year apart and fought like a couple

of puppies. Always had. Lexi was only two years older than Jessie, but lately felt more like twenty-eight going on sixty. With their father gone now, and their mother living in Palm Springs with a distance from the family she enjoyed far too much, Lexi felt like the parent half the time.

Alone at last, she spread her toes in the sand and enjoyed the feel of the tiny grains sifting through like silk.

The Scandal, in a way, was the best thing that had happened to Lexi. She'd wanted to get off the hamster wheel of life on the road. That lifestyle wasn't healthy, eating at all hours of the night, and weird sleep patterns. Never time to sightsee in any of the many wonderful places they had been because they'd been too busy rolling in and rolling out. Next city. Next show. It became easy to fall into sleeping all day and being up all night. She was convinced that way of life had cost her far too much already.

For too long, the Wilder Sisters had supported the entire family, and then some. But Lexi didn't care if she ever stepped on a stage again. At the moment, she was busy ignoring offers to collaborate. Miranda Lambert was interested in writing with her. Sugarland wanted to see anything she had available. When *Falling for Forever* went to number one, suddenly she was a hot commodity as a songwriter.

She supposed she had Luke to thank for that. He's ripped her heart out seam by seam, but hey, he'd also been responsible for making the song popular enough that her half of those royalties were partially helping sustain their floundering B&B.

Frankly, being a songwriter was much more her jam. Behind the scenes. Unlike Sabrina, who'd been their lead singer, Lexi was an introvert who only tolerated public life.

She had hoped she could be happy here in Whistle Cove forever, working at the Wilder B&B with Gran and writing songs. Unfortunately, the songs weren't exactly flying off her guitar. She had nothing. Zip. It wasn't like she didn't regularly try to pry open the creative well and write something. Anything. But she was as dried up as tumbleweed. It was as if she'd never even written a song before in her life.

The pressure to write another chart-topping hit had sliced through her, taking with it her joy to create. But she simply had to remind herself to relax and tell a story. A song with a story that cracked every one of a listener's emotions like *Falling* had. Highs and lows. No need to worry about a hit. A solid song would always find a home. That's what she told herself, anyway.

Unfortunately, the B&B was suffering with too few reservations. Lexi counted on the royalties from *Falling for Forever* to help pull them through the past few lean months. This summer had been their worst on record. Not something she wanted to think about right now, when she should be relaxing. Selling a few more songs to Nashville would further help her Gran and the family business.

Which meant she *had* to write. It was all she had to offer. But like any good writer, Lexi knew how to procrastinate.

She'd write a song...later.

DURING EARLY AFTERNOON wine and cheese hour at the B&B, Lexi found Gram and her new boy-toy, the Clint look-alike. She hadn't been introduced to the man yet, and that was not going to fly with Lexi. Making a big show of bringing out another bottle of Chardonnay for their small group, Lexi dropped by the loveseat where Gran sat.

"Hello." Lexi spoke directly to the man who had his hand on her Gram's knee. Her bad knee, Lexi might add. "We haven't met."

The man, who had to be at least eighty if he was a day,

stood. Very old school of him. Lexi wasn't too jaded to give him points for that.

"How lovely to meet you. You must be Alexis." He bowed. Bowed!

"Um. Everyone calls me Lexi."

"I'm sorry, honey," Gran spoke up. "How rude of me. I meant to introduce you to Clint."

"Clint? Your name is *Clint?*" Lexi said, barely suppressing a laugh.

He smiled, and look at that, he had all his teeth. "It is."

Gran did laugh, a lovely tinkling sound. "What a coincidence, isn't it? It's funny how much they look alike."

Gran's Clint shook his head. "I truly don't see it."

Lexi thought he did have a passing resemblance to the movie star, but every word that came out of his mouth sounded far more on line with Sir Ian McKellen. He was obviously as British as the Queen. After all, Monterey Bay had a large population of European expats, mostly British. Most people believed it was due to the similar weather.

"It's nice meeting you," Lexi said, pleased he had made the first cut. Sir Clint was definitely not a rapist or a throat slasher. Her Gran was safe.

Lexi turned to go but Gran stopped her. "You might want to welcome our new guest. Apparently, someone has already taken the latest vacancy. Jessie checked him in earlier. Said to tell you to come see her, because she needs to talk to you first."

"Why would she need to talk to me?" It wasn't as though she handled any office work. That was Jessie's role.

Gram simply shrugged.

"I'll go talk to her," Lexi said, excusing herself.

She'd talk to Jessie later. Right now, she had a date with her guitar. Her guitar, and the gently lapping waves. It was too cold for Sabrina, Jessie, and most guests once the sun had set, and the classic Monterey Bay fog rolled back in. Neither one of her sisters realized that she'd found her true private time in the late afternoon during wine tasting. After wine tasting, couples occasionally drifted out to the beach. Small, cozy bonfires were started in their private beach safety pits, and at that point Lexi retired to her room to write. Or try to write. Music and words usually came to her at the same time. Lately, nothing would come, but she was sure that would change. All she needed was one song to break through the drought.

Lexi made her way to the private access leading to the former service quarters and her cottage. She'd grab her guitar and head to the beach before everyone else joined in. It would be a beautiful sunset tonight. She could feel it. Maybe she'd write a song about the sunset. People liked sunsets, right?

"Lexi Wilder."

She recognized the deep voice, the smooth sound of whiskey if it could speak. Lexi whipped around to face Luke Wyatt. Her heart hiccupped at the sight of his long and lean body braced against the side of her cottage. One corner of his mouth tipped up in a half smile, and he studied her with those deep, fathomless dark eyes.

Her mouth was dry. Knees? Liquid. "W-what are you doing here?"

"Wasn't going to give you the chance to say you didn't want to see me." He moved away from the side of the house and took a step toward her. "Tour's over. I'm home."

Despite her churning gut, she found her voice. "We have no vacancy. You'll have to stay somewhere else."

He went brows up. "Just checked in."

When she didn't speak, but simply swallowed and blinked, trying like hell to regain her balance, he filled in the silence.

"Still mad at me. Still won't talk to me."

She was so not prepared to deal with this today. With *him*. "Why would I be mad? You mean because you wrote an entire album all about *our* private life? Every single private and personal thing about us. After everything I've been through with Sabrina. No, why would I be mad about *that*?"

"Baby," he said, squaring his shoulders. "It's what song-writers do. We write about our life, the pain and the joy."

"*I'd* rather keep my private life *private*."

"I'm sorry," he said. "I was hurting. You wouldn't take any of my calls. You wouldn't come see me."

"You didn't seem to be hurting. You were all over my TV set, cozying up to gorgeous models and reality TV stars."

She'd seen the woman practically on Luke's lap at a tele-vised awards show. And he was mad she hadn't called *him* back? If he'd been hurt when she stopped taking his calls, he sure in the hell got over it quickly enough.

He took a step toward her making her take one back. *No, no, no.* Already she felt her body buzzing from being this close to him for the first time in a year.

"Give me a break, Lex. You know what this life is like. I didn't even *know* that woman."

Lexi did an internal face palm. No, no. It would not go this way. Check her out, letting loose with all her pent up hurt and anger the minute he showed up, giving Luke every indication of how much she still cared about him. If she didn't care at all, maybe the rumors of these women wouldn't bother her so much. She'd already blown her cover in the first twenty seconds of seeing him. *Get a grip.*

She'd expected to do much better than this if she ever ran into him again, say in Nashville, while visiting Miranda Lambert to collaborate on some songs. Lexi would have another hit song by then. Maybe she'd be dating another handsome country singer *not* named Luke Wilder. She'd be over him by then.

Chalk it up to running into him so unexpectedly, but this wasn't how it was supposed to go. He shouldn't still look so good to her, his beard making him look like a strong mountain man. Like a man who would take care of his woman.

For Luke, it turned out his career came first. Not her.

But the thing to do here was pretend it didn't make a difference whether he stayed or left. Pretend he had that little effect on her. Maybe it wasn't too late to salvage what little was left of her pride.

"I'm sorry." She shook her head. "I'm being rude."

He quirked a single brow. "Yeah?"

Score one for Lexi. She'd shocked him. Good.

"Of course. You're a paying guest and I'm usually not so...so..."

"Pissy?" He gave her another smile, this one lifting both corners of his mouth and demonstrating he still had the power to render her speechless when he laid on the *charm*.

"Yeah. Pissy." She let out a half-hearted fake laugh and waved hand in the air. "Rough day. You know how it is. Sisters."

His brow furrowed. "And how's Sabrina doing?"

He'd had a front row seat to the implosion of the Wilder Sisters, after all. Even though their demise as a band had meant his opportunity for stardom, Lexi didn't doubt he'd been sorry about the way it had all happened.

When she'd been worried about Sabrina, whose entire life from the time she'd been ten had been the stage, Luke had held Lexi every night until she fell asleep, assuring her that Sabrina would survive this. They all would. And she'd fallen even deeper for the man. Luke reminded her there would be life after all the speculation and rumors. Because Luke Wyatt knew a lot about scandal. He understood what it was like to feel like you had to apologize just for being allowed to breathe the same air as everyone else.

"She's okay. Still walks around with ear buds in all the time, singing and dancing. It's in her blood. But I don't think she wants to get back up on a stage anytime soon. None of us do."

He nodded, as if he understood all too well. "And you. Are you still writing?"

Not with you.

Never again with you.

The wall was still up and there it would stay. If anything, she'd wallpaper it. But she was a Wilder first and foremost, and yes, they could put on a show.

She shrugged and got ready to lie. "Here and there."

"I'm supposed to write a few more hit songs." He held up finger quotes. "They want me back in the studio next week. I thought I'd come here and relax. See if I can find some inspiration."

His gaze took a slow slide down the length of her body, and she almost felt...naked. She was so *not* going to be his inspiration. Not this time. He'd taken enough material from her already.

She took a breath and went for deep sincerity. "I hope you find what you're looking for, Luke."

And with that, she opened the door to her cottage and closed it in his face.

CHAPTER 3

"You'd be wise to just relax and accept the crazy." ~ Meme

exi woke the next morning after a rough night alternating between restless dreams and erotic thoughts. She obviously needed a lobotomy because her erotic dream had starred Luke. She'd been on their old tour bus again, strumming her guitar, when he'd taken the seat next to her, holding the prized Gibson he loved so much. He'd given her a sly wink and an easy smile, his gaze dropping to her lap. It was only then that Lexi realized she was stark naked.

"Nobody look at me!" She screamed, holding her guitar up for cover and running to the back of the bus as the entire crew got an eyeful.

"You're mine, baby." Luke joined her in the back moments later. "Only I get to see."

He kissed her then, long and deep, hot and lingering.

"I'm so lucky." He tipped her chin to meet his gaze, and his eyes told her he meant every word.

Then he'd sweet-talked her into bed, the place where they'd always done some of their best work.

Gah!

As usual her dreams were mired with her craziest fears and a kernel of truth mixed in for extra confusion. She'd never been naked on the tour bus in front of the crew (thank you, God,) but Luke had certainly said those very words to her. Many times.

How did I get so lucky?

After working hard to put him in her rear-view mirror, one in-person appearance, and he was headlining her dreams again. It would be much tougher to ignore him for the next few days. But she could do this. Sure she could. All she had to do was hang on for a little longer. He'd be gone just as surely as he'd left on the tour without once looking back.

He'd apparently had what he needed out of her— a #1 song. She'd been left behind in the dust. Not that she'd wanted to go on touring and performing, but she hadn't imagined how much it would sting to watch her boyfriend become the next big thing. What it would be like to run across memes about his fine ass and hard body all over the Internet. What it would be like to know that women everywhere were after him. Relentlessly.

Lexi hadn't ever been a jealous person before, but she'd become one. And she hated herself for it.

As if it hadn't been bad enough to know every women (and some men) seemed to want a piece of her man, she hadn't expected how fame would change Luke. But he became too busy to answer her texts or take her calls. She'd often have to check his website just to see where he was in the country that day. But the last straw had been the rumor that he'd left a show with one of his many female fans—this one a beautiful reality show contestant and big fan of country music. There'd been photos of them together.

Luke insisted none of the rumors were true and that she, above all people, should understand how gossip got started. But Lexi couldn't let it go, and by then they'd been apart for so long (which, okay, was somewhat her fault,) that she didn't know if she *could* believe him. She'd constantly picture Luke enjoying the company of other women, and her helpless and too far away to do anything about it.

Out of sight, out of mind. Beautiful women were everywhere, clamoring for his attention, and whether or not he wanted to admit it, Luke enjoyed that attention. It was in his eyes and in that smile she saw far too often in her dreams. The trust they'd shared for so long, first as friends and then lovers, had shattered. Sudden fame did that to relationships. Families were destroyed, loyalty was tested, and even music took a back seat.

Because fame took everything real and beautiful and turned it into stardust.

Reminding herself that she was an independent woman that didn't need a man to confirm her self-worth, Lexi showered and dressed for the day. Her shower drain was plugged again, and she made a note to phone Tony, their on-call handyman. Thankfully, as Olga the cook's husband, he worked on the cheap.

The Wilder Sisters B&B was a sprawling building situated on the edge of the beach with small service cottages surrounding the perimeter. The main house, constructed in the early twentieth century, contained eight rooms that frequently remained unfilled. Most of their few renovation funds, what little there were, were directed to the rooms that made them money. The small service cottages that surrounded the B&B, and in which she and her two sisters lived, were often neglected.

It wasn't as if the Wilders were rolling in Nashville wealth anymore. They were sort of house rich and cash poor. Their father, John Wilder, an enterprising man, had invested in one too many failed ventures and lost most of their money other than a small nest egg he'd left their mother. Many, including Gran, believed he should have taken better care of his daughters' futures. But Lexi didn't fault her Daddy, gone three years now after a massive heart attack. He'd worked hard in those early years to find them paid gigs, review contracts, and make sure her songs were protected. But today, royalties were nothing like they used to be in the days before streaming music. When their touring stopped, so did most of the money.

Now, Gran's business was struggling to stay relevant. If not for Lexi's royalties from *the song*, she, Gran, and her sisters might have to sell the business that had been in the family for decades. But half of the royalties from a hit song weren't going to keep them afloat forever. Lexi had to come up with more songs, and the sooner the better. She thought of it as her job and duty. Not much fun anymore, but it had to be done, along with the towel folding and sheet washing.

After going for her regular morning walk along the beach cove and counting her blessings (none of which involved Luke) Lexi headed to the large utility kitchen. The only meal they supplied was breakfast, but supply it they did. A large spread with Olga's award-winning scones, muffins, pies, and one delicious hot dish a day. They were about as well known for their breakfast as they were for their spacious, classic rooms with clawfoot tub baths and private access beach.

Olga Hernandez was their baker and all around cook extraordinaire, not to mention supplier of the best coffee in Whistle Cove. Lexi didn't know the secret, but the coffee she roasted and brewed in her personal kitchen coffeemaker always beat the stuff they served their guests.

The aroma of Olga's sugary cinnamon rolls was enough to drive Lexi out of the foulest of moods. She headed to the kitchen to banish away her erotic thoughts of Luke. It occurred to her that if she kept to her current schedule of early to rise and early to bed, she would miss seeing much of Luke. She doubted he was off the tour bus schedule that turned everyone into a vampire. Hell, even Sabrina wasn't totally off the schedule and rarely graced them with her presence before noon.

Lexi walked into the kitchen to say good morning to Olga and pour herself a cup of Java. She ran straight into one of her erotic dreams.

Luke stood halfway up a ladder, and she didn't know what he was fixing, but hers was broken, too. He wore a tight long-sleeved gray Santa Cruz tee with the sleeves pushed up his muscular forearms. A pair of well-worn jeans hugged his fine butt.

Lexi swallowed hard. A familiar heat pulsed through her, winding its way down, and wrapping around the back of her knees.

"But my favorite one is *Can't Sleep.*" Olga fanned herself. "Ay, Dios Mio. When I hear that song, I want to go find Mr. Hernandez and have my way with him."

Luke chuckled. "Glad you like it. That one is a favorite of mine."

Not hers.

Definitely.

Not.

Hers.

"What's going on?" Lexi said, forcing some edge into her voice.

"Mija! Did you know that Mr. Luke Wyatt is staying here with *us?*" Olga said.

"I heard." She made eye contact with Olga, silently communicating to tone the worship down, then glared in Luke's direction. "What's he doing up there?"

"Oh, Mr. Wyatt is fixing the overhead light so I can see better."

"Call me Luke," he said to Olga. "And I'm happy to help."

Lexi leaned near Olga. "I didn't know you needed a new bulb in here. You should have said something. Why didn't you call Tony?"

"Don't bother. I don't need a new bulb, but what's the harm?" Olga whispered. "Look at him."

Luke came down the ladder and Olga elbowed Lexi. "Go thank him."

Lexi shook her head and started to say no, when Olga literally shoved her in Luke's direction, and she wound up two inches from his solid wall of chest. Her skin tightened. Her heart ached.

"Um." She took a step back so she wouldn't bump into him and glared at Olga. "Thanks so much. We don't usually have our guests do *chores* around here."

"Yeah, but I'm not just any guest."

He was so close, that she felt a familiar tug of longing rise up and body slam against her heart. "No, you're even less likely to be asked to help around here. You're a country music star."

"And I'm no stranger to hard work." His tone had a clip to it.

"Well." She stared at the ground before meeting his eyes. "Thank you again. Olga really appreciates it."

"And you?"

"What *about* me?"

Did he want her to say that *she* was grateful he'd replaced a light fixture that didn't need replacing? That she was ecstatic he'd come to their B&B to write songs?

"You don't appreciate it." He pinned her with a powerful gaze.

"Don't you tell me what I think. Of course, I appreciate it.

24

Thank you so much. You're a prince and all that." She turned to go but he caught her elbow. A sharp tingle rippled across her arm when his hand skimmed down her elbow to her wrist.

"Hey, I might as well do stuff around here. I don't want to sit around on my behind all day."

"You're here to relax. And we have a handyman on staff. Tony, Olga's husband."

"Tell you what. If I can't fix it, then you call Tony."

"Wonderful!" Olga said, clapping her hands. "We're so grateful to see that you're still a humble man. Not afraid to get your hands dirty."

Luke flashed a megawatt smile, and Olga blushed a deep magenta.

"Fine. If you'll excuse me, I'm going to make myself useful."

Lexi stormed out of the kitchen, leaving Luke with the new president of the Luke Wyatt Whistle Cove Fan Club.

* * *

LUKE HADN'T EXPECTED a red-carpet reception from Lexi, but he also hadn't been prepared for the Arctic freeze. It was far worse than he'd thought it would be, and his gut pinched with the thought he was too late to win her back.

At least he'd won over Olga. So far Jessie, too, had been welcoming when she'd checked him in, but being the family peacemaker, he'd expected that. He hadn't yet run into Mrs. Wilder or Sabrina. Those two were the wildcards. Add to that Kit Wilder, Lexi's mother, but she was living in Palm Springs with the distance she wanted and the warm weather she craved. She'd never been a fan of Luke's, and he assumed nothing had changed in that regard.

If Lexi refused to talk to him, for now, he'd find a way to

relax and write. The week wouldn't go to waste. Already, he felt calmer simply being home, the smell of the familiar sea he'd grown up around welcoming him. He could breathe again without Gary filling him with encouragement and false praise. Secretly expecting a platinum album this time, and their early retirement. He was everyone's cash cow, and he felt milked.

One thing he never had to fear from Lexi. She was going to cut him exactly zero slack. Always had. Always would.

But hot damn, she looked good. Long blonde hair falling around her shoulders. Striking amber eyes the color of fine scotch. The skirt she wore today showed off her long legs that teased him to distraction. It had taken him all of two seconds to forgive her. She probably didn't think she needed his forgiveness, but she did. He'd been angry for a long time because he'd assumed the trust they had would be stronger than gossip and innuendo. Bigger than long separations.

Rarer than his meteoric fame.

Something told him it would take her a hell of a lot longer to forgive him for ignoring her. For taking her love and trust for granted and failing to see how he was losing her bit by bit.

But hey, he might actually have an entire album written this week if he kept up the pace. Then, he'd get back into the studio and at least hit country gold. He hoped. Platinum would be great, sure, but he'd settle for gold. No need to expect too much.

Late in the afternoon, his back hurting, and feeling rolled inside out from being up so god-awful early to impress Lexi, Luke headed to his room to grab his Gibson. Since everyone else seemed to be inside during wine and cheese hour at the B&B, maybe he could find some solitude on the private strip of beach. Find inspiration from the salty air and crashing waves. He found an empty seat on a blue Adirondack chair, leaned back and strummed, working on the melody he'd come up with earlier. Words would come later. They always did for him.

Good thing too, because he was afraid this song would be another Lexi would want to hang him by the balls for writing. He was feeling sorry for himself again. He'd had plenty of loss in his life, and he recognized he was in no position to be unhappy now. He should be the happiest fool this side of the Moon. His biggest dream had come true, and now he had money and success.

Lexi blamed him for writing songs about their separation, but he wrote his lyrics from the heart. He'd thought she'd done the same, but apparently not. *Falling for Forever* would have been better named *Falling until you Screw Up*. When she'd stopped taking his calls and urged him to "have a nice life," he'd felt chewed up and spit out by the woman he'd loved since he'd been a randy twenty-year-old and she'd spotted him in the crowd.

Yeah, he'd enjoyed the attention he got from beautiful women, but that wasn't love. Even he knew that. And he'd never acted on the numerous forward advances. He'd seen the photos, and understood what it must have looked like to her, because he'd definitely been on the other side of that when she'd been the one in the spotlight.

He forced himself to concentrate and move past the bitterness. This chord progression on the bridge wasn't working for him. Maybe he needed to switch it up. He tried that for a bit until he heard a rustling sound behind him and turned. Lexi stood near the bluff, guitar in hand. She stared at him like she was a gnat on a fresh piece of fruit. Completely unwelcome and a little disgusting, too.

He waited for her to say something like "get the hell of my beach, you bum," but instead she shook her head and turned to leave.

"Lexi, wait." He scrambled off the chair.

She stopped and slowly turned. Her eyes were what had drawn him in when he'd first met her. They didn't know *how* to lie. Right now, they were telling him that she was hurting, and he wanted more than anything to fix it. To sweet-talk her out of her clothes. Get her in bed, where he could prove to her without any words exactly how he felt about her. How he'd always feel about her because even in one long year nothing had changed for him. Nothing.

But that wouldn't happen because this time, he was the loser responsible for the pain he clearly read in her eyes.

"What do you want?"

"Is this your spot? I'll leave if you want some privacy."

She took a breath, as though considering it. "No, it's okay. You stay."

"You could stay with me."

"No."

He snorted. Couldn't help it. "Why am I not surprised?"

She pinned him with a glare. "Don't."

"What, Lex? I'm not the enemy. Stop treating me like I'm a fucking leper."

"I'm not doing that."

"Aren't you?"

"I was really *nice* to you this morning."

"Okay. You made your quota for the day?"

She sighed. Loudly. "I can't do this with you right now."

"When?" He wanted an answer. With only a week, he was on a timeline.

"I don't know yet."

"You're going to have to deal with me. I'm not going anywhere. I'll be there for the next week, so find me when you're ready to talk it out. If you don't, I'll find you."

"Look, you may not have realized it, but you coming here…it's going to bring media attention back to all of us just when the scandal mess has finally died down. We haven't had anyone try to contact us or follow Sabrina around for an exclusive in a while. Now *you're* here."

"Won't let that happen."

"And I don't know that you can help it. Or do you not realize what a big deal you are?"

"Didn't come here to cause you trouble. Believe that." He straightened, pushing down the frustration down a notch. "I wish you'd let me help you. I could pay off some of the loans that are on this place and give you all some breathing room."

She opened her mouth. He was sure she would cuss him out for even suggesting it, but then a couple came towards them.

"Excuse me, but my wife says you look like Luke Wyatt, the country singer," said an older man holding his wife's hand.

Time to pull it together, and be the nice guy these people from out of town expected. Not the bad kid from the docks. Not the kid with a sealed juvie record. Not the grown man who'd fight with his fists if forced.

"It's you, isn't it?" The woman said. "*Falling for Forever* is my favorite song. What are you doing here in Whistle Cove?"

"This is my hometown, ma'am," Luke said, giving both of them a big smile. "How are you all doing?"

He talked with the couple for several minutes about his album and the yearlong tour he'd just completed, his long-ago spine injury aching more with every passing minute. A gift from Reggie that just kept on giving, year after year. He posed for a photo and signed an autograph. All things he expected to do for his fans, even if at times it did interfere with his personal life.

Done with his duty, he turned back to Lexi. But she was already gone.

CHAPTER 4

If I cut you off, chances are you handed me the scissors. ~ Meme

*L*exi hightailed it back to her cottage. She supposed she'd lost that spot on the beach for a short time. Fine, she'd let him have it. Maybe he needed it more than she did. After all, it was a perfect place to come into contact with his eager public as they floated out for a walk along the beach. Maybe he could sell tickets.

Listen to her, sounding so bitter and mean spirited.

She hated the jealous woman she'd become. Screw him and his piercing gaze and melt-your-panties-off voice. He wanted to act as if they could pick up where they'd left off. Well, guess what? They could *not*! She wasn't being unreasonable, no sir, and even if she was, she didn't want to hear about it.

The suggestion that she'd take money from him was outrageous. She would solve her family's problems without his help.

"Lexi!"

This time it was Gran calling for her, standing on the

deck, and waving. Lexi headed back in the direction of the B&B.

She stood at the bottom of the steps to the deck, looking up at Gran. "What's up?"

"Honey, are you all right? I heard." She put her arms out as if Lexi would surely need a hug.

Gran must mean Luke, of course. She didn't need a hug, but she went into Gram's arms anyway. "I'm okay."

"How about him? How's he doing?"

"Luke? I didn't ask."

"Honey, you know this has got to be difficult for him as well."

When Luke had left town a few years ago for his first tour with them, a handful of residents thought that the Wilders had better watch their backs. He was Reggie's son. He might steal all their money and take off to Canada or Mexico. Some place that had no extradition laws.

That boy's no good. He won't amount to anything.

It's like he's an apple that fell from a rotten tree. What can you expect? A bunch of nasty worms, that's what!

Gran had never believed a word of it, same as Lexi and her father. Then again, Gran had always had a heart as big as the Pacific Ocean.

As for Lexi, she didn't know about her heart anymore. Some days she wondered if she had one anymore, but then Sabrina would randomly come up and offer a bear hug, or Jessie would, and Lexi remembered love. Tenderness. From the moment Luke had arrived, she was afraid that she still loved him somehow. This kind of love didn't just disappear. It grew over years and spread like tentacles over a beating heart. But she didn't want to love him, and there it was. Loving him again was too much of a risk.

"He seems fine to me," Lexi said, wondering if that was really true. She didn't *know* Luke anymore. "Reggie's friends are certainly not going to stay here. Jessie wouldn't let them even if they tried."

"I doubt he's going to be able to stay here the entire time. He has to eat lunch and dinner somewhere, doesn't he? He's bound to meet up with some of his enemies who still work the docks."

That was true. The B&B only served breakfast. Of course, she had a small kitchen in her cottage and could certainly offer him some food. She didn't know what it said about her that right now, she'd rather see him starve.

It says you're a bitter woman, and sooner or later the songs are going to dry up if they haven't already. Stop. Just stop.

"If there's one thing I know about Luke it's that he can take care of himself. And maybe you haven't considered this, but his being here is going to bring us attention we don't want," Lexi said.

It had taken the better part of a year, but finally photographers and bloggers had finally stopped coming to town on the chance they might catch another indiscreet photo of Sabrina to sell to the highest bidder. The nude photo published all over kingdom come had earned the seller six generous figures. It would be a wonder if Sabrina ever took her clothes off again, but one thing for certain: she'd never text a naked photo of herself to a man she'd been flirting with over text messages from the road. A man she'd met at a recording label party whom she believed she could trust. Her beautiful and naïve little sister had never met a stranger. Unfortunately.

Gran shook her head. "Sabrina made a mistake, but we've all forgiven her and moved on."

"Forgiveness is one thing, but being forced to relive it is another."

"Are you worried about Sabrina or yourself?"

Lexi shook her head. "One of the reasons I love it here is

that it's quiet and peaceful. I feel safe here. Now we have the biggest star in country music staying with us."

"It's a week. I can see why you want your privacy, but we must still welcome him. After all, it's up to us Wilders, as the hospitable people that we are, to make sure we set the tone for everyone else."

That was obviously a dig at Lexi. "What did Olga tell you?"

"She said you seemed to be angry with Luke."

Had Gran forgotten how much she'd cried over him? "*Gran!*"

"I know you decided it would best for the two of you to be apart, but that doesn't mean you should be *rude*. You're the face of Wilder Sisters B&B. We all are."

Yes, God forbid a Wilder be rude! On the other hand, at the prices they'd been forced to charge for their rooms just to break even, they couldn't afford to lose a single customer who was willing and able to pay.

Lexi bit her lower lip. "Right."

"Besides," Gran said. "He could have stayed anywhere else, but he's here. There's a reason for that, honey. I bet he still loves you."

Lexi ignored that. "You're right. None of this means that I have to be *rude*."

"That's my girl."

After giving Gran a kiss on the cheek, Lexi headed back to her cottage. Once inside, she set her guitar in its stand by the black kettle wood-burning fireplace. The cottage wasn't much but it suited all her needs. A one-bedroom, she had one hallway that led to the small kitchen at the back of the house, one tiny bathroom, and a small living area in the front which was separated from the bedroom by classic French doors. The entire décor said *beach* from the weather worn book case painted sky blue to the wood paneled walls in the bathroom.

She'd stuck a loveseat and her guitar stand near the kettle fireplace for the cold nights. It was a fact of life in Whistle Cove that nights were chilly even during the summer. Now they were headed into autumn and that chill would fall on them and pierce with its sharp sting. She didn't have anyone keeping her warm these days, which was just fine with her. It didn't matter that Luke had always kept her cold feet warm, or that he'd always slept with one arm slung over her waist and she'd never felt safer. She didn't need that anymore.

Lexi made herself a shrimp salad for dinner, wondering what Luke would have. He'd probably gone into town to get some of his favorite clam chowder soup by the wharf. Either way, it wasn't her problem. After dinner, she tried her hand at writing again but came away with nothing. She didn't know what she would do if she didn't come up with something to demo soon. Her few contacts in Nashville wouldn't wait forever, and she couldn't afford to miss this opportunity.

When a soft knock sounded on her cottage door, she hoped it wasn't Luke. She didn't want to write with him again, and she could sense he was about to suggest it. Who wouldn't want country gold to strike twice? He might not need her for much else, but they'd created something special with one song. It was only human to want that again. Which might be exactly the reason he'd come here in the first place.

Warily, she opened the door slowly to find her sister Jessie behind it.

"Hey!" Jessie pushed past, followed quickly by Sabrina bringing up the rear.

Jessie carried a paper shopping bag. "I brought desert."

"And I've got a movie," Sabrina said, grinning and holding up a copy of *P.S. I Love You.*

Oh snap. Just what she needed. A tear-jerker.

Desert was a molten lava chocolate cake from the *Death*

by Chocolate bakery in town. Lexi's favorite. "Wow. Thanks. What's this about?"

It wasn't like they didn't often get together and eat themselves into a sugar coma, but that was usually while watching the CMA Awards. Or a Chris Hemsworth movie.

"Because I hope this isn't about Luke," Lexi said as she pulled out spoons from the utensil drawer. "Gran and I talked about it. I'm okay with him staying here. It's only a week."

"Oh, yeah! We know you're okay," Sabrina said. "You're so okay that you can't listen to the radio. But now, he's right here at the B&B, and you're just super."

"I am!" Lexi protested, desperate to believe it. "This morning, I caught him helping Olga in the kitchen. He looked really good up on that ladder, all manly and muscular with his sinewy forearms, and you know? I didn't even care."

"Yeah?" Jessie handed everyone a spoon. "That's good to hear."

"Sure, it's good to hear," Sabrina said. "But too bad it's not true. Sinewy forearms? How can we just let her get away with this?"

"Get away with *what?*" Excuse her, but Lexi thought she'd done very well not drooling over Luke, thank you very much.

"With your incredibly humongous boat load of denial!" Sabrina accused.

"Okay, first of all, that's what we songwriters like to call hyperbole. And I'm not in denial," Lexi said.

"No?" Sabrina went one hand on hip and wiggled a finger. "Then let me give you the 411. The fact that you didn't care about how hot he looked this morning? The point is, you *noticed.*"

"Anyone would! So did Olga, and she's a happily married woman." Lexi wanted this to be true. She hadn't noticed those brawny arms and broad shoulders, for instance, because she was still in love with him. She'd admired them because she wasn't blind. End of story.

"Hm. She has got a point," Jessie said and absconded into the bedroom with the cake.

Jessie was wise. She knew how to get people to follow her. Lexi and Sabrina did just that and flanked Jessie on either side of the bed to dig in.

"Which one of us has a point?" Sabrina asked, licking her spoon. "Me, right?"

"Both of you do." Jessie pointed to Lexi and then to Sabrina. "She's right that anyone would notice, and you're right that she noticed. See how I did that?"

"That's some of your best work, Jess." Lexi sighed.

They didn't call Jessie the family mediator for nothing. The chocolate was warm and sweet and gooey. It slid down her throat like a sparkly, silky dream. Maybe she should think about marrying this cake instead of a muffin. So much sugar, so little time...

"So, are you ever going to like...forgive him?" Sabrina said.

"Ooh, good question!" Jessie turned to Lexi.

"First, he's not going to be around that long. Second, I don't have to forgive him. I've moved on. See how I did that?" Lexi rolled her eyes.

"Except that if you had *really* forgiven him then maybe you wouldn't still be so angry." This was from Sabrina, always wiser than she looked.

"Let me see if I can explain this." Lexi would have thought the two people who knew her best in the world would buy themselves a clue, but okay. She'd help them along. "Look, Luke is famous right now. And I don't know if you guys considered this, but his being here, even temporarily, is going to bring us some attention."

"Maybe that wouldn't be such a bad thing?" Jessie said. "I mean, we have vacancies to fill, and that would do it."

"As long as they're coming here to see Luke, and not just to look over our...okay, my train wreck," Sabrina said. "We've had enough of that."

Lexi would have to agree. She'd enjoyed this past year, living in the quiet and solitude of the beach. Now that Luke had chosen to grace them with his presence, how long would the peace last?

"I'm happy for him, but I don't want to be near that crazy tour and performing schedule anymore. He's going to live the rest of his life very much in the public eye, and I'm not. Ever again. He and I want different things now."

"Okay. That makes sense. I have to admit it." This from Jessie, the voice of reason.

"But how do you know you both want different things if you won't talk to him?" Sabrina said.

"Huh. That makes sense, too," Jessie said.

"And you're both awesome songwriters. You write beautiful music together," Sabrina continued.

A fleeting thought occurred that she didn't want to believe or accept. Pain sliced through her at the thought maybe he'd come here for another hit song. From her.

"We wrote one great song." One awesome song. Luke had the melody and she'd come up with words straight from her bleeding heart. "And I want to try writing on my own again for a while."

"Hey, I'm sorry I was nice to him yesterday when I checked him in, but you know me," Jessie said. "I have a hard time being mean. If you want me to hate him, I'll do my best."

"And I'll bring it home because I have no such problem being mean. We'll hate him together. Sister power!" Sabrina held out her free hand for a fist bump.

Lexi returned it. "I don't want you to hate him. But it's nice that you offered."

Jessie and Sabrina had her back. Always would. And she would have theirs. Once, Luke had her back too. But it was different with her sisters. They'd endured five nights a week of band practice for years, a few teenage heartbreaks, outdoor performances in the Bay Area way before country music was popular in the Bay Area, ten tours, five albums, and of course, The Scandal.

It was safe to say that if she didn't hate her sisters by now, she never would. If Lexi had nothing else, she had Jessie and Sabrina.

And for now it would have to be enough.

THAT EVENING, Luke decided he was starving. For affection, for attention from Lexi, and also for some actual food. Hindsight being twenty-twenty, he probably shouldn't have come to the B&B. There were plenty of other places he could have stayed, some that might even have appreciated him. He'd been a little too optimistic coming here, which quite frankly didn't sound like him at all. Now, he was too tired and hungry to be positive, so he immediately rejected his first inclination to ask Lexi to dinner. He wanted to eat with her, wanted to talk to her, wanted anything with her at this point. Because he missed her like his right arm. Missed talking to her. Missed her advice and honesty. Missed her back rubs, and...missed a lot of other things, too.

He climbed in and started up the rental, a BMW sedan that Gary had waiting for him at San Jose International Airport when he'd arrived. Luke felt ridiculous driving the car. It would be the car for a lawyer, or a real estate agent. Not for a country musician. Luke had wanted a truck or an

SUV, but one hadn't been available. He would even have preferred his old green Ford Ranger pick-up, which had ripped seats and happened to have a lot of pleasant memories attached to it. On second thought, best to keep those thoughts away.

Traffic was light as he drove to the wharf and parked. He wasn't concerned anyone would recognize him as a star. Country music wasn't all that popular in Whistle Cove, and his fame was new enough that, unless one caught the weekly country countdown on CMT channel, they wouldn't know who he was at all. Even so, he'd brought a Giants baseball cap he pulled low on his head. There might be others who would recognize him for a very different reason.

His past on the wharf involved being on the other side of the docks. Working alongside Reggie since he was twelve or so, he'd been on the supplier side, bringing in the catch of the day. He'd rarely been the customer and certainly not from any of the more expensive restaurants. If he had anything at all to worry about, it might be running into one of Reggie's friends in town. Those people who had insisted Reggie was not guilty of murder, and Luke was nothing but a bad son. He didn't fear any of them, hadn't even when they'd threatened him for testifying against his father.

Luke shook his head clear of the past. The ghost of a raw and painful memory was alive and well here, but it couldn't touch him anymore.

He walked by the expensive restaurants lining the pier, offering the best seafood, along with tourist trap gift shops for everything from kitchen magnets to fleece sweatshirts. The taffy shop that displayed the taffy rolling through the old-fashioned machine in the front pane window was still a personal favorite of his. Lexi also loved the saltwater taffy here. He found himself inside the shop, where he ordered an assorted flavors bag. The teenage clerk gave him funny look, but Luke paid in cash, hoping she wouldn't be able to figure out where she might have seen him before. She was too young to know him from his days working the boats alongside Reggie.

Carrying his bag, he walked the pier feeling more alone than ever. Success wasn't supposed to look like this. Shouldn't he be happier now that he had money? He hadn't signed up for this raw emptiness he felt churning in his gut. Hadn't realized when he'd signed a contract, recorded an album, and left on a tour, that he'd lose Lexi. The one person other than Maggie, his mother, who'd always believed in him.

He'd gotten busy, and let's face it, somehow screwed up his priorities. Not like he'd ever known what success looked like so it hadn't been easy to handle fame when it arrived. The attention, from beautiful women in particular, had been addictive and flattering. Before Lexi, any woman worth the trouble wasn't interested in him. If they had been it was because they were slumming it. Rich Bay Area girls who liked to piss off daddy with the local bad boy who had a record for street racing.

He continued to walk along the pier, trying to shake off the memories that lingered. It was a slow night on the pier in the middle of the week, and some waiters were standing in front of their establishments with samples of crab and shrimp cocktails, trying to lure patrons inside. One even had a coupon for 10% off.

"Sold," Luke said when the waiter offered one to him.

Didn't matter how much money he had, safe to say he'd always like a bargain. Without thinking, he removed the ball cap and followed the waiter to the back of the restaurant, where he was seated at a table facing the window overlooking the boat dock. Luke's first job had been cleaning shrimp from the nets of his father's boat. Not where he wanted his mind to go right now. Memory cells were cruel.

"I'm sorry, but you look so familiar." A woman at the table next to him turned to stare. "Are you...oh my God, aren't you *Luke Wyatt?*"

"Yes, ma'am." He smiled and nodded.

"I love your music! Especially *Falling for Forever.*"

Color him surprised that was her favorite. Not. "Thank you."

He signed an autograph on a cloth napkin, posed for a selfie, which led to many more photos with some of the other customers.

"Let him eat!" The waiter finally said and then slipped him a slip of paper to autograph. "For my sister."

Luke ordered the clam chowder and a lobster tail. He wasn't going to drink, but people kept sending them over. First a German beer, then a glass of local Cabernet, and champagne flutes on the house. It would be rude not to accept, so he drank some from each. By the time he finished eating, paid, and took a selfie with the cook, Luke thought he might have to be rolled out of the place.

Holding his bag of taffy, he strolled to the BMW, evaluating his condition. No, he wasn't shit faced. But he was *something*. Clearly, he couldn't drive back to the B&B. What most residents didn't know about him was that he was far from being a bad boy. After a few mistakes as a stupid teenage kid, he'd mostly toed the line with authority. You didn't grow up in the shadow of a man like his father and not learn a thing or two. Luke didn't take chances with the law anymore. Ever. He rarely drank and never smoked. All he needed was to get pulled over and fail a sobriety test and not only would he be indeed his father's son, but he'd be the country star with a drinking problem.

Cue the man in black, everyone, for round two. He was

already compared to a modern Johnny Cash who sounded like Thomas Rhett. The record label had packaged him that way to sell records.

It was working.

He broke out in a cold sweat just thinking about jail, just thinking about being his father's son, and whether the son was doomed to repeat the mistakes of the father. He pulled out his cell and dialed Lexi.

This time she actually picked up. "Luke?"

"Yep, it's me. I need a ride because in my current condition I shouldn't be driving. Do you also perform that service for your guests, or should I call a cab?"

Silence for a moment, then she spoke.

"Just tell me where you are, and I'll come get you."

CHAPTER 5

"If you mess with the big sister, there's always a younger, crazier sister right behind her. That's who you don't want to mess with!" ~ Meme

hen Lexi pulled into the wharf's parking lot, it didn't take her long to find Luke leaning against a blue sedan. His arms were casually folded in front of him, and he gave her an easy smile when he caught sight of her truck. *Oh, boy.* How exactly did he manage to look sexy and badass even when she had to come rescue him?

She'd been a bit unnerved having to come to his rescue at the wharf. He might have run into some of his father's friends here. One thing about Luke she understood. He refused to show fear to anyone. Coming to a stop next to him, she unlocked the passenger door of her truck, and he folded his long legs inside.

"Can't beat this. Curbside service." He handed her a white bag from Mrs. Merry's, the saltwater taffy shop on the pier. "For you."

"Thanks. You didn't have to."

"Peace offering. And force of habit."

She pulled out the parking lot, giving him a sideways glance. He didn't seem drunk to her, but then she realized that Luke toed the line with authority. More so than most people for obvious reasons.

"We'll send someone to get your car tomorrow."

"Didn't want to take any chances. Lots of people buying me a drink tonight. Cause I'm so wonderful and all."

"You got recognized." That didn't surprise her, but relief flooded through her that the experience had been completely positive, and he hadn't run into any of Reggie's men.

"By a few." He twisted in his seat, and she wondered if his back hurt. "Some just gave puzzled looks."

"Reggie's friends will leave you alone," she said, and hoped. "You did the right thing, and now you've made something of yourself. No one can argue that."

He snorted. "They'll try."

"Then let them. They don't matter."

"But you matter."

She squirmed, feeling his gaze on her, making her warm. Like tiny little pinpricks of light pierced her skin. "Don't—"

"I know. You don't want to hear it. But I'm sorry, Lex. I ignored you. I didn't put you first. There's no excuse for it. You didn't deserve that."

She sucked in a breath at the raw memory, as painful as the exposed nerve of a tooth. But before tonight, he'd never apologized. Only made excuses.

"I know what it's like. All the fame and attention. Everyone loving you and wanting a piece of you. Of course, it's different for women because men aren't exactly throwing their boxers up on the stage or waiting backstage for a hook up," Lexi said.

"Maybe not, but the musicians are."

His jealousy had flared hot every time she'd had to spend

time with a male musician not part of their band. "I don't know about that, but I thought the success we earned after so many years of hard work was nice at first, and then it got… overwhelming. I couldn't breathe."

"Why didn't you ever tell me that?"

"I didn't even tell my sisters. It was my job to sing and write and perform, and I did love that. I didn't like the lifestyle."

"Comes with the territory."

"Exactly." She slid him a significant look.

It wasn't *her* lifestyle anymore, and he was still in the thick of it. She'd never be able to blame Luke, not matter how hard she tried, for riding the gravy train until it broke down. He deserved a chance to make a life for himself in the music industry, and he'd worked hard for everything he had.

"I get it. We can't ever be together again because I'm still touring. Is that what you want to tell me?"

"That, and we can't be together because you broke my heart and…well, it's been a *year*, Luke."

"Why? Are you seeing someone? Have you changed? I mean, other than the fact that you're not touring anymore."

"That's not really the point." He'd made her uneasy now, pushing against her tight defenses.

"What is the point?"

Lexi pulled into the B&B and her parking space in the service area near her cottage. She shut off her truck and turned to him. "Maybe I don't feel like I know you anymore."

He leaned forward to tuck a stray hair behind her ear. "You know me, baby."

"I know that you hurt me. I know that."

"Lexi, honey—"

"No. It's not going to be that easy. You can't just show up here with your guitar and your hot body and sexy beard, and get me back in bed with you."

He rubbed his chin and grinned. "You like the beard?"

Shit. She hadn't meant to spill her guts. "Yeah, it's okay."

With that, she hopped out of her truck before the false intimacy of close quarters made her tongue any looser. She'd already put body and bed in one sentence and could only hope he hadn't noticed.

But two seconds after she'd stepped out of her truck, it became obvious he'd heard her loud and clear.

"Don't walk away from me."

Just outside the door to her cottage, he stepped into her. She drew in a ragged breath at his nearness. Her poor heart did a pirouette and a swan dive. She didn't want this intense longing for him, but the rest of her body hadn't yet received the memo.

Instead she obviously enjoyed being nearly plastered against his body because she hadn't backed up. He smelled so good. Like sandalwood soap. Like leather.

Anytime now. Just take a step back, and he'll get the message.

A corner of his mouth tilted up. "About the bed thing—"

She squeezed her eyes shut. "Can't we just forget I said that?"

"Not a chance." His eyes studied her, hooded, dark, and filled with warmth and longing.

He was killing her.

"Maybe we're not headed to bed, but you could learn to trust me again."

Why? So you can just take off again and leave me behind? So you can use me?

"You're going back to Nashville." She turned her head, unwilling to look at him when he was this close.

"Not right now." His hands slid down her arms and cuffed her wrists.

His palms were rough and calloused, bringing back good memories of those hands. All over her. They could be tender too, and coax the deepest sighs of pleasure from her lips. Then she did step back, because she couldn't take any more of the contact without jumping out of her tight skin.

She wasn't going to Nashville with him.

"You want to be friends again? All right, you got it. I'll be your friend."

Only seconds from the safety of being inside and away from all his heat, she heard his low and deep voice right behind her.

"Didn't say I want to be your *friend*." His arm braced on the door behind her. "Your sisters are your friends. I'm your man."

"Listen, I'm cutting you some slack because you've had a few tonight. But you *were* my man. Past tense." Why was her voice shaky? She cleared her throat, straightened and put some steel in her spine.

"Sounds like you need reminding. I'm back now, and I can remind you."

Remind me. Those two words had meant something special and intimate to both of them once.

She swallowed back a sob at the ache reflected in his shimmering eyes. She'd seen that pain before but this time she couldn't help him. This was the way break-ups went. She'd welcome him to her club, but she was sure he didn't want to belong. They were both hurting but it couldn't be helped. She could get over him if he'd give her a little more time. They could and should both move on.

"I believe I told you I can't do this with you now." She glared at the arm braced next to her, at his powerful forearms.

After another second, the arm came down slowly. "Got plenty of time."

* * *

FRIEND ZONED.

Such a good feeling. His heart was raw and felt like an apple she'd just taken a bite out of. Luke stalked away after Lexi shut her door. The desire and ache coursing through him now meant now might be a good time to write a song, but there would be too many four-letter words in it. She might have kicked him deep into the friend zone, but Lexi was mired in the denial zone. That became obvious the moment he'd heard the hitch in her breath when he stepped into her personal space. Testing. And the eyes that never lied to him were telling him too much. Like the fact that she still wanted him in her bed, even if she didn't want him in her heart. She couldn't just wish *that* away.

His phone buzzed in his pocket and he pulled it out. Gary again. Luke was surprised he'd given him a couple of days without checking in.

Generous of him.

"Yeah?" Luke tried to push the irritation out of his voice. Gary was bound to take the anger personally when it had nothing to do with him. "How are you?"

"Good, buddy. Just wanted to check in with you. Can I set a meeting for you here in Nashville in another week or so?"

Luke had said a week. But he would need more time. Besides, the songs were coming now. No words yet, other than ones full of resentment, but they were decent melodies he could work with.

He looked up to see tonight's sunset, a splash of orange and crimson red. *Red sky at night, sailor's delight.* A similar sunset to the first one he'd caught with Lexi years ago on their first official date about seven years ago. They'd been friends first before they'd become lovers. But now he knew what it was like to kiss those sweet lips. To hold her naked body next to his. Hell no, he wasn't going back to the friend zone.

Not without one hell of a fight.

"Might stay here longer."

"How long we talking?"

"Whatever it takes. The songs are flowing. Can't stop now."

"Can we be a little more specific? I need to book studio time. And having a date I can give the guys will make them feel confident you'll be back."

"Seriously? They doubt I'm coming back?" The idea there was any question he'd be back hit him hard. These people had no faith in him.

"Not like it hasn't happened before. You're off the reservation and stranger things have happened. Some artists can't hack the pressure of fame and walk away from it all."

Pressure. They ought to try the pressure of testifying against a father for murder. Touring and recording weren't real pressure, and being in Whistle Cove again reminded him of that simple fact.

Luke cleared his throat. "That's not me. You can tell them that. I'll be back, and you can be sure of it."

He'd never allow it, no matter how much weight was pressed on him, threatening to squeeze out any creativity he had left. This future he'd built wasn't just for him, it was for Lexi, too, if she'd have him.

"I know that, bud. You've worked hard to get here."

"I'm thinking a month. That should be enough time." His gaze drifted to Lexi's closed door.

Time enough for *what* he didn't know. Maybe time enough for her to kill him. Or maybe time enough for her to change her mind. He couldn't just walk away and cut his losses.

Not when it came to her.

"Alright, I'll hold them off here. Assure them that you're coming back with some hits."

He raked a hand through his hair. "Hey, Gary? Think you can lay off the pressure for a hit? I'm writing *songs*. Good ones, I hope. I sure can't guarantee they'll all be country gold."

"Sure, sure. We all understand that. The thing you need to realize is that you're blazing right now. Hot as a damn jalapeno pepper. You could put anything out, and your fans will buy it."

Huh. Not too flattering. Maybe Gary was just trying to make him feel better and ease the stress, but Luke didn't like the idea of putting out anything less than his best effort. Once he hung up with Gary, Luke wandered back to the B&B, not in a hurry to get back to his lonely room. It was a beautiful room with all the comforts, naturally, and all of the rooms were. His was named *The Sea Captain*. Everything in blue nautical themes. A comfortable and roomy Queen-sized bed he'd be sleeping in alone in for the foreseeable future.

He walked along the beach after the sunset, losing track of time and enjoying every minute of it. Like old times, nights Reggie had kicked him out of the ramshackle cottage they shared, forcing Luke into being a sometimes beach bum. But much as he'd wanted to leave home, he couldn't leave his mother behind. So, he'd always come back to protect her.

When he got back from his walk, he noticed Mrs. Wilder and a man dancing on the deck in the soft moonlight. Without music.

Hell's Bells. Looked like Mrs. Wilder might be getting some tonight. Somebody might as well. He was happy for her and the man who looked to be eighty-something. It was high time for Luke to say hello and face whatever kind of reception he'd get from Lexi's grandmother. He had to assume Lexi had more than bent her ear about how he'd changed since getting his big break. How he neglected to return calls and texts. Maybe she'd even seen the photos of him and that chick whose name he could barely remember.

"My darling, even with your sore knee, you have the grace of a prima ballerina assoluta," the man said in a heavy British accent.

Luke didn't know what the hell that was, but by the look on Mrs. Wilder's face, he laid odds the compliment would get this man laid tonight. He was about to go around and give them their privacy when he heard Mrs. Wilder voice.

"Luke."

He turned to see she had her arms wide open. Of all the welcomes he might have expected or hoped for, not one of them had been with open arms. Of course, he went for the hug, while the man next to her smiled and nodded.

"My friend, Clint." Mrs. Wilder made the introductions.

"You're pretty smooth there, sir," Luke said, shaking the man's hand.

"Why, thank you." Clint bowed.

"Luke's an old friend of the family." Mrs. Wilder hooked her arm through Clint's. "And quite a successful country star. He used to play in the girl's band, and now he's on his own."

Luke agreed that was the short version. "I owe everything to the Wilders."

"Oh, no you don't, Luke." Mrs. Wilder touched his shoulder. "You're very talented, and my son noticed that immediately. You would have been a success either way. I'm just glad we had a part in it."

But if not for the Wilders, Luke might have fulfilled the very low bar set for him. He'd already been on that path until the day he'd run into a show on the wharf. Three sisters had been performing for anyone who would listen. They were damned good, all of them, but he hadn't been able to take his gaze off the tall blond with the amber eyes. She played the guitar and performed with such ease, that he envied her.

"I hope we've been kind to you," Mrs. Wilder continued, "Are you happy with your room? Is everything to your satisfaction?"

He nodded, wondering if he might arrange with management to have a certain amber-eyed woman deliver him breakfast in bed. "Perfect."

"You must try the blueberry scones," Clint said.

"I will." So far, he hadn't hit the breakfast spread they offered since he usually skipped the first meal of the day, preferring to sleep through it. "You two have a nice evening."

He walked a few steps before Mrs. Wilder caught up to him alone. "About Lexi. Please excuse her. I heard she was rude."

"She wasn't—"

She held up a hand to stop him. "I know my granddaughter. She's very bullheaded when she gets an idea in her head. Think how she must have felt seeing you with that beautiful woman. When you wouldn't return her calls—"

"Mrs. Wilder, I'm sorry about that photo, but I never would have hurt Lexi. It was a rumor."

She smiled. "I know exactly how these things go. Lexi does, too, but she's too close to the situation with you. She can't be objective. At least not yet. Call it youth, or pride, I don't know. But she's convinced herself you two would be better off apart."

"And you don't think so?"

"I don't *know*. I'm old enough to finally realize I don't have all the answers. Yes, that's the benefit of old age! Exciting, isn't it?"

"Yes, actually."

He'd love some of the peace that surrounded Mrs. Wilder. The knowledge that you didn't have all the answers but that was okay. Because sometimes he still felt as if he couldn't run hard enough or fast enough to get where he needed to be.

Now that he'd reached a pinnacle of sorts, what would it take to stay here? Seemed as if it would never end. Every time he reached a goal, someone moved it higher for him.

Her wise eyes softened. "Sometimes...these things need a little time."

"I can be here for the next month, but then I need to get back to Nashville."

"I understand. You have obligations. The girls have been there."

Reason number one he thought Lexi should understand. Once they'd been the sole support of the Wilder family. Lexi knew what kind of pressure Luke was under. People depended on his success. It was no longer about him. No longer about the two of them and the life they'd once planned together.

He shoved his hands in his pockets and hunched a little against a strong bay wind. Unlike Mrs. Wilder and Clint, he wasn't dressed in a sweater.

"Still care about her."

Try you're in love with her, you damn fool. It's the kind of love that you can't get over.

"Don't give up."

CHAPTER 6

"Sisters don't let you do stupid things...alone." ~ T-shirt

The next morning Lexi showered and noted her tub drain was still clogged. She thought Tony would have come by to take care of it already and made a mental note to remind Jessie, who usually scheduled this sort of thing. Lexi spent the morning washing towels and sheets and folding them. Towels and sheets were the armpit of owning a B&B, and next time she was going to get Sabrina to help. She didn't do enough around here.

Sabrina always got the fun jobs, like schmoozing with guests when she managed to get up in time for breakfast, and later during wine and cheese hour. The born entertainer in her came out then, laughing and chatting. They all adored her. The perfect hostess. Meanwhile, Lexi and Jessie got the worst jobs. Jessie was good at organization and management. Checking guests in, confirming reservations, scheduling repairs. Keeping guests content. Lexi was good at the hard work no one else wanted to do. Kind of always had been that way. At least the mundane and repetitive work gave her plenty of time to clear her head and think, because she might be good at this but it didn't mean she enjoyed it.

What *would* she enjoy?

She took a moment to remember last night and Luke's hard body pressed up against her. Invading her personal space. And her not objecting to said invasion. What was wrong with her, anyway? Her body had experienced a disconnection with her brain. It sure picked a bad time for that. All her body had allowed her brain to register for the moment was how good it felt to be touched again. Not just any touch. Luke's. And she wanted him. All of him. She was ticked off about that.

What she really wanted was to stop feeling like twenty-eight going on sixty. For this past year, she'd done nothing but stand still while everything around her had continued to move. Her old life was over, but she wasn't even sure her new one had begun. She wanted to stop feeling sorry for herself and everyone she'd lost. She wanted to listen to *Falling for Forever* without crying.

Whatever else Luke did to her, he alone made her feel alive and young and crazy. She missed that. He was the only man she would trust with her body, if not her heart.

So maybe they could just fool around a little bit in the short time he'd be here. Then he'd be off and out of her life again. It might not hurt if she was prepared for it to happen. And if she was careful, really careful, she could keep her heart out of it.

No, no, no, said her brain! But the sound was muffled when her body put her brain in a chokehold.

You go ahead, hon. We've got this, said her body.

Remind me, he'd said. It was code. He'd once said, remember that time we didn't get out of bed for two days?

Not really. Remind me.

How about that time you made me late for sound check?

Remind me.

She missed having a man look at her the way Luke did. As if he wanted her as his breakfast, lunch, and dinner. Like she was still first with him. She doubted that was true, but she could be the only woman for him right now. Why not? Unlike other people in Luke's life, she didn't want or need anything from him. She didn't need to write another hit song. She didn't need her first big break. She didn't need to have a photo op with him to advance her career.

All she needed was his body.

All I want is your body.

Oh! This was it. She had the start of a new song. The melody came flowing out seconds later along with the words, a sexy tune about a one-night stand. Unlike anything she'd ever written before. Sassy. Might be her new image. Could be. She dropped the last folded towel in the pile and ran in the kitchen for a piece of paper and a pen. She wanted to get this down now before she lost her inspiration.

"Quick! Where's a pen?"

"In my kitchen?" Olga just looked at her. "What for?"

"Do it! Just give it to me."

Oh, that was good too. It was going in the song. Quick. Pen. Paper.

"Never mind, I'll ask Jessie!" She half ran, half jogged to Jessie's office.

"Jessie! A pen! Now, please."

Jessie went through desk drawers. "I…I guess I don't have one."

"You don't have a *pen*?"

"Don't look at me that way. I do most everything online. Why don't you use the note feature on your phone?"

That wasn't funny. Jessie knew very well Lexi had stopped carrying her phone around with her everywhere because of all the constant alerts. Tweets. Facebook PMs.

"You need a pen! And paper. Back to basics. I'll be in my cottage if anyone needs me."

"Now? But wait a—" Jessie called out.

Nope. No time to chat. A song was 2% inspiration and 98% determination, and if she didn't hurry she'd lose her 2%. Lexi jogged towards her cottage. She not only had good old-fashioned pens and paper there, but her guitar. With this kind of inspiration, she might nail it all down in one sitting.

A song. Finally.

She threw open her unlocked door, even though she could have sworn she'd locked up this morning. Running to her guitar nearly out of breath, she collided into Luke's chest.

"Whoa. Where's the fire, girl?" He righted her, dropping strong hands around her waist.

She was eye-level with his pecs. "What are you doing in my house?"

Thoughts were powerful, so she'd been told again and again, but this was ridiculous. Surely, she hadn't conjured him here.

Don't ask. Just give it to me. I want your body.

"Never mind. I can't talk to you right now!" She pushed against his rock-hard chest, and the rock finally moved.

Paper. Pen.

She scribbled down every lyric that was running through her head at roughly the pace of a Kentucky Derby champion. In her process, the melody was so tied to the words in her mind that she'd remember it. Even so, she picked up her guitar and strummed a few chords. She lost track of time, so it might have been an hour or a few minutes, but finally she had the entire song down. First, second and third verses. Chorus. Bridge. The first draft, anyway. Something she could work with and fine tune until it was exactly what it needed to be. When she put her pen down and glanced up, Luke was studying her with those intense mocha eyes. He didn't break eye contact with her.

He hadn't even tried to stop her or slow her down by asking questions because he understood.

"You good?" He said now.

She stared with dismay at his utter maleness, even while wearing a flannel shirt over a tee, and immediately went into hospitality mode as a force of habit. "I'm sorry, can I help you?"

A slow smile slid across his lips. "Yes, you can, but that's beside the point. I fixed the shower drain."

"*That's* why you're here."

Made sense. Not conjured up at all by her thoughts. He was here doing his good deed for the day. Yay. It had occurred to her that he was perhaps subconsciously trying to atone for his transgressions with hard work. He couldn't be more obvious.

"Luke, you don't need to be our handyman. We have one."

He lifted a shoulder. "Jessie asked me."

"Of course she did."

She could yell at Jessie, but it was clear that she'd tried to stop Lexi. Warn her what she'd be running into. And this happened to be exactly what Lexi had wanted a few minutes ago. Luke, only a few feet away from her bedroom. It wouldn't be that difficult to push him a few feet in that general direction, to the other side of the French doors, and her bedroom. The woman in the song she'd just written had a lot of guts. She was a strong, feisty, and independent woman who only needed a man for one thing. But she also wasn't afraid to tell a man exactly *what* she needed and wanted from him. And leave her heart and the silly promises lovers made to each other out of it.

But the author of the song wasn't feeling quite as confident. Or maybe just a little gun shy. It had been a *really* long time.

"Yeah," Luke said now. "Should have told her to call Tony for you."

"No, no. That's—that's okay."

He quirked a brow. "Last night you couldn't get rid of me fast enough."

Lexi stood up so suddenly she misjudged the distance between them. At some point, he'd moved closer. She pushed him back, one hand on his chest, directly over his heart. *Too much, too soon,* her brain screamed. *More, more,* said her body!

"Sorry. I was just being honest," Lexi said.

"I'm the one who's sorry. We're friends if that's all you want from me." Then one corner of his mouth tipped up in a smile, his dark eyes glittering with mischief. The same smile he gave when he knew something she didn't. Good news, usually, like a Grammy nomination. She had a feeling this wasn't going to be good news, at least not for her. "But you left something out."

"What did I leave out?"

His gaze dropped to her lips. "You want me."

She thought about her song, which with every passing moment grew to be less wonderful to her and more like a song that tried too hard. A song that wanted to be sexy, bad, beautiful, and liberated. All the stuff that Lexi wasn't. Yeah, this song wasn't going to work.

"Ha! Don't get ahead of yourself. You haven't yet been named People's Sexiest Man Alive."

"You think I care about that?" One hand covered the nape of her neck and tugged her even closer, so they almost shared a breath. "Just want one woman to think I'm the sexiest man alive."

"Luke—"

He studied her, giving her a good long look into his eyes.

The eyelids were hooded, his gaze filled with desire. Longing. "Tell me to stop, and I will."

She didn't tell him to stop. Didn't want him to stop. Instead she rose to the balls of her feet. When his firm lips finally pressed against hers, a jolt of electricity shot up her spine. He was warm and solid and real under her palms for the first time in forever. For just a moment, he was her man again. Again, he was her reason. He was her next breath. A pleasant pulsing ache settled in the apex of her thighs.

She'd forgotten, or maybe had just tried to forget this connection she'd always had with Luke. The rest of the world faded into the background, as it always had before. She'd never cared what her father, or her mother, who'd never liked Luke, thought about her starting up a relationship with their back-up musician. With the son of Reggie Wyatt. Never cared about Luke's past. Every time they touched, she could be on a tour bus in the middle of the United States or on an island in the Caribbean. They could be anywhere, or everywhere. She was surprised to find nothing had changed in that regard.

Which was wonderful and also a huge problem.

She broke the kiss and stared into eyes so hot they might melt her. "I-I just wrote a song. The first one in a while."

Holding her chin in one warm hand, he traced her jawline with his thumb. "I know, baby, and I'm happy for you."

"The thing is I lied to you before. I haven't been writing. Mostly trying to write. I thought I'd be filled with inspiration here, but instead I got...stuck."

He tenderly pressed a kiss to her forehead and then leaned his forehead to hers. Not speaking. Listening.

She stepped back, wanting a little distance and perspective. "I know that when we were together, I probably got too attached. Men and women are different when it comes to intimacy."

He straightened. "Wait. That's what you think? That I didn't get too attached to you?"

"You sure had an easy time moving on."

A small tick worked in his jaw. "I didn't move on from you. Life slowed down for you, but it sped up for me."

Wasn't that the truth. They were on different tracks now. He was the express train, and she wasn't even sure she wanted to be on the track.

She nodded. "And I've been standing still for what feels like a long time."

"Thought that's what you wanted. You didn't want to keep touring. You want a private life and not a public one."

"Just because I know I don't want my old life doesn't mean I'm sure what I want next."

It occurred to her that she'd only become dissatisfied with her life when Luke came into town. He reminded her all right. Reminded her of all the good parts of everything she'd lost. She didn't want to live her life under a microscope, but she missed the connections with other musicians. All the impromptu jams. Her tribe.

"You're just…part of that old life I had. And it hurts a little bit."

He winced and took her hand in his own. "Hurts to see me?"

This was coming out all wrong. "No. I don't mean that. Luke, I'm still trying to figure this out. My entire adult life up to this point was spent on a stage. Traveling. Performing. Some of that was unhealthy for me, and you know that better than anyone. It hasn't been easy to make the change back to normal life."

"Think it's been easy for me? I never wanted all these people depending on me for their livelihood. I lucked into this gig, and you and I wrote a hit song. Now I have to rinse and repeat, and I don't know if I have it in me."

She squeezed his warm hand. "Of *course* you have it in you. Don't think of it as writing a hit song. Just write a good song."

"Until I got here, I wasn't writing any songs at all."

"And now?"

"I'm writing again. Which is the reason I'm staying for a month." He dragged a hand through his hair. "I know I told you I wouldn't be here too long. But I want to stay while I have inspiration."

A month. He was going to be underfoot for a month. Staying. Playing guitar in her spot on the beach. Fixing anything he could fix and reminding her of her old life. A life she missed, and a man she wanted. Both taunting her to make up her damn mind. Make a choice.

"Don't they need you in Nashville?"

Yes, that's right. Go ahead and re-direct. Nashville needs you.

"When I come back, I'll have some songs and we can go right into the studio and record."

"I'm sure it will be another gold album."

"And what if it's not?"

"Don't you dare feel sorry for yourself, Luke Wyatt. If it's not country gold, the world won't end. We toured for years without hitting gold. You already have your audience, too, those who will stay with you through thick and thin."

He let out a gruff laugh.

"Missed you. You always believed in me. You're the only one who's straight with me. The only one who won't lie to me or tell me what I want to hear. You tell me when I'm cutting corners. When I'm not giving it everything I've got. When I believe all my bad press *and* my good press. When I'm hurting and need to slow down."

"How's your back?"

Luke had injured his spine years ago when he'd stepped between his mother and his father and taken flying lessons.

He'd done that many times, but when he was fourteen, it had caused an injury that was still with him to this day. It was one of the reasons her father had taken him off the road crew and accidentally found out Luke knew how to play a guitar. Because, though he'd never once complained, the pain was obvious on his bad days.

"It's fine." He pulled her back into his arms. "Do you want me to show you?"

A bad back had certainly never stopped him from having an incredible amount of stamina and agility in the bedroom. *Not* that she was thinking about that right now. Ahem.

There was a light knocking on her door. "Lexi?" Jessie's soft voice.

Lexi froze. Luke didn't let go and tightened his hold.

"Maybe she'll go away," he said, kissing her neck.

"She won't." Lexi sighed.

"Damn, wish I hadn't wasted so much time talking."

Another knock, and Jessie's voice louder this time. "Is Luke still in there? Because there's someone here to see him."

CHAPTER 7

"In our family, we don't hide crazy. We put it on the porch and give it a cocktail." ~ Meme

Luke wasn't interested in whoever was on the other side of the door. It could be someone with another autographed Gibson originally owned by his hero, Garth Brooks, and he wouldn't care. This had better be important because he'd been close to Lexi's bed, close to being inside her again, and that's something he did not take lightly. She'd let her guard down today enough to trust him enough and give him the crap that he needed to hear. Coming from her it meant everything. He'd live another day if he didn't hit country gold again. Lexi was right. She always had been. He needed her next to him on this crazy ride. But she was done with that part of her life, just when he was getting started.

He should have known he couldn't be lucky enough to have both of his dreams.

"Be there in a minute," Lexi called out and tugged out of his arms.

He didn't make it easy for her, grabbing on to her elbow and then her wrist as she moved away from him. "Damn, you didn't even try. They might have gone away."

She shook him off, but a sweet smile was tugging at the corner of her lips. "You don't know my sister like I know my sister."

When Lexi opened the door, it was to Jessie with a woman Luke didn't recognize. Lexi moved behind him.

"Hey, guys? This is Tracy Ballard from *Country Music Today*." Jessie introduced the blond next to her.

She was young enough to look like a fresh-faced idealistic college kid and carried something with her that looked suspiciously like a camera bag. He'd seen enough of them in the past few months and wasn't exactly thrilled to see one now. Bad timing.

"I'm sorry to interrupt, but I saw your Friendbook feed. You've been tagged on so many photos from the area that almost everyone knows you're here."

He was pretty sure he heard Lexi lose all her air, deflating like a popped balloon. So much for his anonymity, but obviously he'd been an idiot to think he could hide anywhere in the social media age. Everyone had a Friendbook account, even grandmothers.

"I tried to tell Tracy that you're here on vacation, but she said she'd spoken to your label and they agreed to a photo shoot while you're here." Jessie worried a fingernail between her teeth.

"They didn't tell me about it." Then again, it wouldn't be the first time he'd missed a communication from the top. He'd signed with Rise Up records, an independent that had recently been acquired by a larger corporation and been out of the loop since then. But he would have thought he'd at least hear from Gary first.

"I'm sorry," Tracy said, giving Lexi a sideways glance, "But

I drove up from Los Angeles. Long drive, especially in traffic. I'd hate to go back now without some photos."

"Wouldn't want you to do that." Luke smiled, stepped outside, and turned on his show persona.

Lexi none too subtly closed her door behind them. If that wasn't a message, he didn't know what was. This was his life, he now understood, and separate from hers.

"I didn't mean to…um, interrupt," Tracy said, not looking the least bit sorry.

"No problem," Luke said.

"I'll leave you to it." Jessie walked away.

"Mind if I check with my manager first?" Luke pulled his phone out of his back pocket and started walking away from Lexi's cottage.

"Of course not," Tracy said, looking back to the now closed door. "Was that…is that Lexi Wilder?"

"The one and only. This is her family's B&B." He punched in a quick text message to Gary that contained a few four-letter words in it.

"Sure, I had heard that. That would make such an interesting story. The two of you here in Whistle Cove. I could—"

"No," Luke interrupted her. Worried it sounded like he didn't want to share the limelight, he corrected himself. "Lexi needs to be left alone right now, and that was part of the deal with my staying here."

"I assume Sabrina is here too, then?"

Shit. He figured she'd already know that. "Yeah, she is, and she also values her privacy."

His reply text from Gary was apologetic, but he'd been out of the loop as well. He would check with the label but advised Luke to be gracious and welcoming.

D-uh.

Problem was he hadn't intended to bring unwanted attention to himself *or* the Wilder sisters. Lexi was roughly as protective of Sabrina as a Mama Bear with her cub, so he hoped for Tracy's sake that she wouldn't intrude. Not coming up with a way to casually drop this without sounding like an idiot, he instead took Tracy through a short tour of the outside of the B&B and proceeded to talk up his small hometown.

"A long way from Nashville. It's beautiful here," Tracy said, taking out her camera. "I've always loved Monterey Bay. It's unusual for someone like you not to live in Nashville. Isn't it? Usually we've got all the rockers in Cali."

"I'll be going back to Nashville." He decided not to mention that the Wilder Sisters had never officially moved to Nashville. Somehow, it had worked for them. But that had been a different time. A time when John Wilder had ruled. He'd get his way or his daughters wouldn't sign the contract. He had that kind of pull. And he'd always kept Whistle Cove their home base.

Tracy snapped shots of him walking away from the private beach into the public and along the way bending to pet a friendly black Lab.

"I never had a dog growing up." Wouldn't have wished any pet on Reggie Wyatt.

"You should get a Lab. He seemed to like you."

Two hours later, he'd talked about the gold album, and lied about his break-up with Lexi being the inspiration for the songs for the hundredth time, when Tracy threw him her first personal question. These were always easiest to answer because he didn't actually have a private life since Lexi had dropped him.

"Are you still seeing the woman from the Ms. Single Executive reality show?"

"Never dated her. It was a rumor. Completely untrue. That's why it's a rumor."

"Someone new then?"

He laughed. "Nice try. But I don't have time to have a relationship when I'm on the road. It's…hard to meet people."

And harder to keep them.

"Really? I would think you'd have to peel the women off you." She grinned, snapping away. "So, you and Lexi—"

"I don't talk about Lexi," he said and put a clipped edge in his tone he hoped got the message across loud and clear.

"What's next for you?"

"A whole new album." He bent to pick up a broken sand dollar. "Working on it right now. Was, anyway."

"We should get some photos with you and your guitar."

He squinted. "Don't you have to get back on the road?"

"I booked a room in town. I didn't want to drive back too late." She glanced at the couples now drifting out to the B&B's deck on to the private beach.

Would have been nice to know that before he'd agreed to this. He had every intention of getting back to Lexi tonight. Hoping he'd get rid of Tracy after the guitar photos, Luke agreed and headed up to his room to find his guitar.

* * *

"How long you think she'll be here?" Jessie asked.

"Hopefully not much longer." Lexi raised her wine glass to Jessie's and they clinked together.

They were both standing on the patio deck of another vacant room. The Mermaid Room. A feminine room in every way, with pink and turquoise undertones, it was possibly Lexi's favorite. In the distance, Lexi spied couples walking hand in hand along the beach. Some of them holding wine glasses, some holding only each other. Luke sat on the Adirondack chair attracting the attention of some as he strummed his guitar while the photographer snapped photo after photo.

Gran was out tonight with Sir Clint. Some kind of charity fundraiser in Carmel, and they would be staying away for a few days. Sabrina was holed up in her cottage, having heard that a photographer was lurking about.

"Am I wrong, or were you and Luke about to make-up?" Jessie said, a smile in her voice.

"No." Lexi shrugged. "I wrote a song, and I was feeling pretty high on that. He was there, I was there."

"Lexi! That's great."

"The song or Luke?"

"Both." Jessie took a sip of wine. "They're both good, right?"

"The song for sure. Maybe I got ahead of myself on the other." She watched Luke now, posing for another photo with a couple who'd stopped to chat.

Despite where Luke had come from, and the hell he'd been through, he'd never stopped reaching out to people. Never gave up hope. She loved that about him, and her heart squeezed as she watched him now. He was good at dropping everything to share with his fans, appreciating them in a way she'd personally seen many artists forget to do. It was incredibly selfish of her to miss the days when she'd been first with him.

"Whatever he did, and I'm not sure he actually did anything wrong, it's clear he's sorry now," Jessie said. "Don't you want him back?"

She'd have to be crazy not to want the man everyone else wanted, right? But she didn't want him because every woman did. Having every woman after him now was his least attractive quality.

"What if he's just here to get another song out of me? We had no idea that *Falling for Forever* would be the hit it turned out to be. And there's pressure for him to hit country gold again."

"I'm sure he can do that on his own. Luke wrote his own songs before you two collaborated."

"Don't listen to me." She bit her lower lip, mortified at how close to tears she'd just come. "It's just that…Maybe I want the *old* Luke back."

Her Luke. The boy who'd taken her on carefree rides in his beat-up Ford pick-up, and who'd taught her how to kiss. The one who'd endured her greatest loss right along with her. The one who'd needed her as much as she'd needed him.

"You mean before meteoric fame? Before the world noticed him?"

"I'm horrible."

She didn't want to hate Luke's well-deserved success, but she missed the simpler times. The times when they both lived in their small town and toured together on the same bus. Close quarters never seemed so attractive to her until after she and Luke had shared a bed.

"Hey, you're not horrible." Jessie elbowed Lexi. "It's a little late to get that Luke back, but for what it's worth, I understand. Who wants every single woman alive trying to get near her man?"

"Someone who doesn't value privacy as much as I do?"

"Maybe." Jessie tossed her hair back, a sure sign she was getting ready to drop some majorly unsolicited sisterly advice. "I sometimes wonder, though, if the hardest pill for you to swallow is the fact that we were once the headliners. Luke was in the background, and he was lucky to be with you. Now most might think you'd be lucky to be with him. Of course, I know *he's* the lucky one if you give him another chance."

Lexi's stomach tightened in response to the truth of that statement. He'd once called himself lucky just to be with her.

Now that he was center stage and receiving the adulation of most women, he couldn't feel the same way. That was okay, she understood. He deserved someone who felt lucky to be with *him*. Not her. It was damaging to a relationship to have so many other people in it. Managers, publicists, employees. So many responsibilities and commitments. She'd witnessed relationships disintegrate under that pressure before. Some of the bands they'd opened for had members who no longer spoke to each other, post-divorce. Now, she and Luke wanted different things. He was enjoying his new-found fame and she'd tired of it all. It wasn't helpful to spend months apart and to want different things out of life. She was simply being logical about this. Mature.

"I don't like it when you read my mind." Lexi shoulder checked Jessie. "Did I mention that?"

"A few times. But I would think you'd be used to it by now."

"There's also the fact that he's leaving for Nashville."

"Not right away."

"Funny, that's what he said. But I don't know if I can trust him anymore."

"Other people in the business make it work."

Lexi quirked a brow. "Do they?" She believed no such thing when fifty percent of marriages ended in divorce. The stats were even higher for musicians.

"I have five words for you: Tim McGraw and Faith Hill."

Lexi groaned. "And they're both still performing. Together."

"But don't you want to play again? Since you were twelve, you've had a guitar in your hands. That's not something you can just dismiss."

"It's harder to play now. Harder than ever."

"Look, I don't know, but isn't all of this worth a risk? I doubt Luke has changed. Look at him. Doing stupid odd jobs around here just to be near you. He's as humble as pie and would still consider himself lucky to be with you. He's still that boy in the back row that saw you as the only thing that mattered to him in the world. Something special. Don't you know how much we all want that?"

"I know." Lexi grabbed her sister in a sideways hug, squeezing tight.

Lexi wasn't the girl in her song sassy and sexy song, and she never would be. She couldn't just have Luke's body and have a one-night stand with him. Or a two-night stand. Or a month-long stand. Not when she already knew what it was like to belong to each other heart and soul.

"Earlier today, I fooled myself into thinking I was the girl in my song. But I'm not and that's the point. I might be able to write a really fun song but *I'm* not...fun."

Gee, how depressing was that?

"Okay, I don't know what you're talking about, but I'm just going to put this out there: why don't you just talk to him about all this?"

"Um…"

Lexi wouldn't voice her fears because they sure didn't make her the bold and confident woman she wanted to be. To say the truth out loud made her sound like a coward. And talking to Luke might lead to kissing Luke, which might lead to…other things, and in the end, her heart would be stomped on again.

She didn't know if she could take that kind of risk.

"If you hurry you can catch him." Jessie made a show of shoving Lexi towards the door.

Lexi stuck out her tongue. "We have very little left to talk about."

"Even better. Save the tongue action for all of the kissing."

"Okay, I'll go talk to him, but I might not say what you want me to."

She went out the door and down the hall, greeting a couple clearly headed back to their room. "I hope you're enjoying your stay with us."

"We sure are," the woman said. "We just met Luke Wyatt on the beach."

"Oh, is he here?"

"He's doing a photo shoot. He's even better looking in person. Go see him! Do it!" The woman urged.

Lexi smiled and headed downstairs. She walked only a few steps only to spy Luke at the bottom, guitar in his hand. He glanced up at her, gave her a slow smile, and her heart cracked open. Just cracked wide open like a walnut. All this before he'd even said a single word. This was a problem because he already had her.

She knew what she had to do.

He came up the steps to meet her on the landing. "That took a hell of a lot longer than I'd hoped, but I finally got rid of her."

"This is exactly what I was afraid would happen. I'm sure she's only the first photographer to get here. They'll be more. I wonder how much longer before everyone knows you're here."

"What am I supposed to do? Want me to send them away?"

"No. I know you need to do this. It's part of being a public figure. But—"

"I get it." He slid his guitar down and held it by the neck. "You want *me* to go."

She couldn't meet his eyes. Didn't want to see any more hurt in them. "Might be best. Don't you think?"

"I don't know. Is it better to have another vacancy when you're already struggling? You tell me." His words were sharp and pointy.

And maybe that had been why he'd chosen to stay at the

B&B in the first place. She should have seen it coming. Luke thought he owed her. Owed the family for giving him his first big break.

Unwilling to take his pity, she straightened her spine and met his gaze. "Is that why you're staying here? Don't worry about us. We're fine."

"That's not what I've heard."

"Jessie is researching us expanding into catering and...I've got offers to collaborate on songs, plus all the royalties from our hit. I'll manage. The last thing you have to worry about is me."

"That might be true, but I wish you'd let me pay off some of the loans you have on this place. Give you some breathing room."

"I've already said no."

His gaze pinned her, dark eyes heating up. Now he was straight up pissed. "You won't even think about it. Do you always have to be so damn stubborn?"

"Yes, I do. And if you came here to help us, please know that we don't need your money."

"Hell, what good is all this money if I can't help the people that mean the most to me?"

A familiar ache sliced through her heart. Luke didn't have any family he could spoil. No brothers or sisters. And Luke's only known living relative was spending the rest of his life in prison for murdering his mother.

"You've earned it. The money you have is yours."

"It doesn't mean anything to me unless I can help someone. You know that better than anyone." He took a step closer and laced his fingers through hers. "Let me help, baby."

"Luke, please." She bit back tears. "I don't trust you anymore. I want you to leave."

CHAPTER 8

"Don't worry about me. I'm going to be fine. I come from a strong line of lunatics." ~ Meme

"Yes, Mrs. Dailey. Don't worry about us. Um, sure. We've locked up all the silver. No, we're fine. There's no need to call the police." Jessie rolled her eyes. "You do realize he has more money that we do. Oh. Uh-huh. I understand. Thank you for caring."

Every muscle in Lexi's body tensed when Jessie hung up. "What did the old biddy have to say?"

It was finally morning, and Lexi had spent another restless night thinking about Luke. She'd hurt him because she'd told him the one thing that would cut him to the quick: she didn't need him. Another lie. A little help would have been welcome. And those strong arms around her, holding her at night? Let's just say she'd never kicked him out of bed before.

"She said a leopard never changes its spots. Or something about a tree and an apple. I wasn't really listening by then." Jessie opened up the laptop on her desk and clicked away. "I told Luke he has to move out of the Captain's Room because we already had that room booked for two nights starting today. I was going to move him to the Mermaid Room, and he said I should talk to you. He's under the impression you want him to leave."

"I decided it would be best if he stayed somewhere else in town. I asked him to leave."

"Why?"

"It's just...hard having him here. Talking to him and kissing him and—"

"You kissed him?" Jessie grinned. "That's great."

"No, it *isn't*. If he'd just give me some more time and distance, maybe I could think clearly. Figure some things out. But when he's in front of me, he's like some bright shiny object that I can't help but want!"

"Oh, yeah. Now we're getting to it."

"And anyway, we both know the press, not to mention all his fans, are going to be hanging out as long as he's here. And we don't need the attention. Sabrina doesn't need anyone coming around revisiting such a humiliating time for her."

Jessie cast her eyes heavenward. "I see. We're going to go ahead and let one of the *hotels* in town take all of our business. That's what you're telling me?"

When she put it that way, it sounded stupid. "But...aren't we basically doing okay for now? What about the catering?"

"That's going to take some time to implement and money we don't really have to invest right now."

Lexi leaned back in the desk chair and gripped the armrest. "I wish you'd said something."

"We're managing, but, since Luke got here, we've filled all the rooms to capacity for the first time since...well, a very long time. I can only imagine why."

Lexi pictured all the sheets and towels and rubbed her forehead. But if business got considerably better, they could hire some more help. Lexi could focus more on her writing. "I see where you're going with this."

"Do you? Because so far, Luke is good for business." She closed her laptop and folded her hands on top of it. "I don't think anyone's interested in Sabrina any longer. Luke is the main attraction. Maybe we just need to get over ourselves. It's been over a year, and Sabrina is not the only celebrity to get caught texting a man with photos of her boobage. Many have done far worse."

Lexi cringed every time it was mentioned out loud. Sabrina and her stupid phone. But even though Lexi could have killed her at one time, she now hurt for Sabrina, who'd trusted a man she shouldn't have.

"Yes, but how many of them were part of a squeaky-clean country music band and wore a purity ring?"

Jessie sighed. "Not many, I'm guessing."

Last night, when they'd converged on Sabrina in her cottage, she'd seemed to be handling the photographer being nearby and all the many new guests beginning to converge, all fans of country music. She was handling Luke's presence far better than Lexi was. Sabrina brought out some of the old outfits she'd previously used for disguises. A black dress that went nearly to her ankles, black hat, and black pilgrim pumps. No one would have ever recognized the Sabrina who usually wore bright blue and hot pink and the cutest shoes ever in *that* outfit.

But no matter how peppy and upbeat Sabrina got, Lexi knew that deep down, her sister had been cut to the marrow by the slut shaming she'd had to endure. Their true-blue fans had stood by them, but people who had probably never listened to their music had turned on them. So had the media. Lexi didn't understand the cruelty. The anger. Now the name-calling had finally ended and Lexi feared a reporter or one of Luke's fans would bring that terrible time up, and it would start all over again. After all, he'd been a part of their band when The Scandal had happened.

But maybe Jessie was right, and Lexi needed to get over her damn self. Their guests found Luke the main attraction, and as long as she and her sisters could stay in the background, what would it really hurt?

She squeezed her eyes shut. "Would it help if I asked him to stay?"

"Only if it won't kill you. I've gotten pretty fond of having you around."

"You know he's going to think I'm crazy. I just asked him to leave."

"I'd say he's pretty used to the Wilder sisters' brand of crazy."

Lexi couldn't imagine what he'd say to her now. No time like the present to find out. It was early, and check out time wasn't until eleven, so she'd get to him before he packed his bags. She swallowed hard over the pebble lodged in her throat and ran up the flight of steps to the Captain's Room. She knocked on the door and heard Luke's deep morning *just woke up* voice. It sounded as if he'd just swallowed a bottle of sexy.

"Hold up. Be right there."

Maybe she should have tried later, like after he'd had coffee and was (she hoped) fully dressed. Her palms were sweaty, so she could try again later with dry ones. "I can come back."

She'd started to walk away when the door creaked open, and she turned to see a sleepy-eyed Luke with bed hair quirk a tired brow. He didn't need to speak at all. The brow said it all for him. She'd heard that brow loud and clear. It had just asked her, "W*hat the hell?*"

Life was so unfair. As usual, he was adorably cute in the morning. Disheveled dark hair partially falling over one eye.

He was the cover of GQ magazine, bedroom eyes edition. He was shirtless. Of course he would be. It was morning, and he didn't sleep in his clothes. Who did? Even she liked to take her clothes off when she slept. Nothing wrong with it. Okay, now she was rambling. Her brain was rambling. And all this before her tenth cup of coffee.

But here was the thing. His body was as perfect as she remembered. He was still all hard planes and angles. A light dusting of dark chest hair tapered down to disappear beneath the sweat pants he wore low on his hips.

"Lexi?"

Crap. She was openly staring. Brazenly, even. Her eyes drifted up to meet his gaze. "Yes."

His lips were twitching. "You need something?"

She shook her head and blinked twice to get her bearings. "I wanted to talk to you."

"Come in." He waved her inside.

She glanced around the room. His guitar was on the unmade bed, along with a notebook and pen. Luke was old school that way, just like her. He grabbed a rumpled long sleeved thermal from the bed and pulled it on. If anything, it made him more desirable.

"I'm calling around to find another place. You're not running me out of town."

"That's what I wanted to talk to you about."

"Yeah?" He folded arms over his sinewy chest.

"I was actually thinking that...here's an idea, and I'm just going to throw this out there. Why don't you go ahead and stay? I mean you'll have to move to the Mermaid Room because this one was actually pre-booked before you decided to stay longer. But if you don't have a problem with that, then I don't have a problem with you staying as long as you want. Or need."

He studied her as if she was some sort of an oddity. Some

new zoo animal he'd never seen before. "Let me see if I got this. Now you're okay with me staying here?"

"Well, we have the room, so I say, what the heck, why not?" She blew out a breath. "You know?"

Boy, this was difficult. She hadn't put on a show like this in a while. Performing was exhausting, and she was out of shape.

He gave her a slow smile because yes, he understood now. Those dark eyes assessed her. He had her. She could only hope he wouldn't punish her family because she'd been selfish enough to want to protect her heart. Because it was too difficult for him to be this close when she still wanted him so much.

"So...you need me?"

"We need you. Yes. The family."

"Not you."

She studied the carpet. "I'm part of the family last I checked."

He walked past her on bare feet, giving her his back as he studied the view from the plate glass window. Below them, white-capped waves rolled in, and morning fog greeted the day. Seagulls squawked. It would be another cold morning in Monterey Bay.

He stayed silent. Not a word.

She kept babbling, a special skill of hers. "All the plans we had...the catering is going to take a while to set up. My songs aren't exactly flowing lately. And we've got a waiting list since you showed up. I don't think that's a coincidence."

Lexi waited for him to say something. Anything. He could toss her out of the room and hurt her twice. Once for her family, and once for herself. She couldn't blame him. But since the first cut had already been made, it wouldn't hurt as much.

Because Luke understood she'd do anything for her sisters. For Gran. For family. And once not long ago, for him.

He turned to her. "Since you refuse my help in any other way, I'm glad I can at least keep the place full."

"Thank you." That sense of kindness in Luke, the fact that he'd help even now, softened her heart and other pink places. Suddenly it wasn't so hard to accept his help in this small way. He, the main attraction, would stay. For now.

A dark and hooded gaze met hers. "But there's a price now."

"Hey, that's blackmailing." But she smiled anyway as he blatantly bribed for her time.

He gave a slow smile. "Have dinner with me. Two dinners."

"Dinner? Why?"

"Because I miss you. And we both have to eat."

She didn't answer while her heart throbbed in her chest. She was half surprised he didn't hear it.

"Two dinners, and if you still hate me, I won't bother you again," Luke said.

"I don't *hate* you."

"You just want me to go far, far, away and never kiss you again."

"I definitely don't remember saying *that*."

"You want me to kiss you?" He gave her a crooked smile.

Put that thing way before somebody gets hurt, she almost said out loud.

She wrapped her arms around her waist. "I don't have an opinion."

"Got it. That's a first." He took a step closer. "Do we have an agreement?"

She took a step back. Some parameters could be put in place for their agreement to work for her, but Luke had never pushed. He'd never once put his hands on her without knowing it was exactly what she wanted. Her body was always safe with him.

It was up to her to guard her heart. "You didn't want to leave anyway."

"Right. But now you need me to stay."

"W-where do you want to have dinner?" She said.

"Anywhere. You get to pick one place, and I pick the other one."

Having dinner with him wasn't going to kill her. It could be a pleasant meal, and they'd catch up on old times. She'd keep it strictly to the music industry. Songwriting and that sort of thing.

"No funny business." She threw that in there just for kicks.

"You know me better than that."

She certainly did. That's what worried her. She gave him her hand, and they shook on it.

"You've got yourself a deal."

* * *

THE ROOM WAS PINK. Oh, excuse him, *mauve.*

Luke threw his bag on the bed and carefully laid his guitar down. Though he'd done his share of hanging around the Wilder B&B when he'd first met Lexi years ago, he'd never stayed in any of the rooms. But he'd certainly heard about the Mermaid Room. It was legendary. He knew it was pink, which was fine, but this room looked like the inside of a Pepto bottle. He occasionally saw the inside of one when he was hung over, and it was a great product. But its color wasn't meant to decorate walls and curtains, lamps and...for the love of God, sheets, too?

Oh, hell no, he wasn't going to sleep between pink sheets. This right here is where he drew the line. He ripped them off the bed, rolled them up in a wad, and stuck them in the bottom dresser drawer. He'd have someone bring him some normal colored sheets. White sounded good. Didn't anyone ever tell the Wilders that there could be too much of a good thing? Like, for instance, *pink*.

He had more time. Two dinners. He wouldn't leave for Nashville without being certain that she was done with him. He wasn't convinced they didn't work anymore. They needed balance. Somewhere he'd read that balance was the key to life. He couldn't and wouldn't give up his career, not now, but he'd seen plenty of musicians with families. All of his current band members, for instance. He figured it took a strong woman to be able to trust in her man. And that's where he'd run into trouble. Lexi didn't trust him with her heart anymore. Maybe he had no one but himself to blame for that.

He sat on the edge of the now sheet-stripped bed. She wasn't going to make it easy for him. Didn't matter. She was worth it.

After a shower and getting dressed, he went downstairs to the breakfast area just before the end of the buffet. After so much talk about the food, even a non-breakfast person like him was going to have to try it. The breakfast nook of the B&B was set up a like a restaurant in that there were many small two-person tables in one large room. One end of the room faced a window wall with a view of their private beach. Breathtaking. The B&B had always been, and still remained, the destination for couples. For lovers. Already, there were dozens of couples seated and enjoying each other's company, if one were to go by the longing gazes as they wouldn't break eye contact with each other.

One woman was so engrossed with the man seated across from her that she didn't notice when Sabrina Wilder came by to offer more coffee.

Sabrina, the *second* wild card.

She sashayed over to him, and he covered his coffee cup before she could mess with his perfect combo of milk and sugar.

"Good morning, Mr. Nashville. Didn't think I'd see *you* up this early."

He sensed a cold front coming in. "Figured I'd check it out. Clint kept going on and on about the blueberry muffins."

"Sir Clint?"

"He's a *Sir*? As in knighted by the Queen of England?"

She shook her head. "I don't know. Lexi calls him that because he's so British."

That made him laugh. "How are you?"

"Not as good as you are. That's for sure."

"You still singing?"

She smiled, probably because Sabrina was the consummate performer. "Only in the shower. For now."

"Shame." He took a gulp of his coffee. "You're talented."

"Nope. That would be Lexi. She's the songwriter and a helluva guitar player."

"No argument from me."

"You should also know that I've decided not to hate you."

"Um, thanks?"

"Lexi didn't want me to anyway, but I make my own decisions about that. I've decided you're okay in my book. We actually have a lot in common, you and me."

He squinted, wondering what he had in common with the coddled baby sister who put the wild in Wilder. "We do?"

"Yep. We both love Lexi, and neither one of us handled all the fame and attention we got too well."

"Ouch." He rubbed his chest like she'd wounded him with a poison dart. "What's a little truth between two friends?"

"Exactly." She turned when she heard someone calling her.

Lexi waved from the other side of the large room and closer to the fireplace, a scowl on her face.

"Excuse me. Duty calls." Sabrina waved.

"See ya."

He continued to eat his breakfast. A hot dish with fried potatoes, chorizo, and bacon was hands down his favorite. Olga was a damned good cook, and he'd have to give his compliments to the chef. Maybe she'd have some recommendations as to where he might take Lexi to dinner. He didn't want it to be any old place. It should be something special and expensive. He could afford it now, so why the hell not. He was in the middle of chewing a particularly crunchy piece of bacon when he saw that the people around him had stopped talking.

At first, he only noticed a teenager nearby openly staring in his direction, but then it was obvious the entire room was looking at him. As he *ate*. He was not a particularly delicate eater, nor was he a slob. But he'd never intended his meal to be a performance. Yet it felt very much like one right now. Worse, it was the way people were staring at him. As if they'd never seen anything like it before. A man. Eating. Honey, grab the camera!

Finally, a young woman approached him, practically tiptoeing toward him in as if afraid to step on a landmine. He tried a smile as she got closer, and she literally dissolved before him. Her hands shook, and she handed him a piece of paper.

"I w-would l-love your autograph."

"Of course." He took the paper and pen. "What's your name?"

"Amanda."

"How are you today, Amanda?"

A blush crept up her neck and spread like a virus over her

cheeks. "Great. I'm here with my family. W-we all love your music. Especially—"

"Falling for Forever?" He finished for her.

"Yeah," she giggled and clutched at her sweatshirt. It read *Monterey Bay Aquarium.*

He signed her autograph, but it hadn't stopped the staring from everyone else. But now, most were smiling in his direction. A wave here. A nod. They behaved as if were different from them all right, but in a good way. Except for the brave teenager, no one else approached him. They simply stared until he caught them and then looked away.

Not the first time some of the residents of Whistle Cove had stared, some of those looks filled with pity and some filled with contempt. But it was clear none of these fans were scared of him.

They were *intimidated* by him.

Unnerved by the feeling of being watched, Luke took his coffee and with a quick nod and smile, headed back to his room to write.

CHAPTER 9

"My family is temperamental. Have temper, half mental." ~ Meme

By Thursday, Luke had been holed up in his room for two solid days. For lunch and dinner, he ordered in from the nearby pizza place that delivered. He hadn't planned to hide out, but he'd noticed with some curiosity that recently the B&B guests had gone from mostly couples to single women. Some scattering of teens with their mothers, and there were still a few couples here and there. But they were no longer the majority.

Yesterday, he'd taken a jog along the private beach to find a group of women following him. When he stopped, they stopped. He started jogging again. They did too. No one would come up and talk to him unless he initiated a conversation by waving hello. And being that many of these were attractive women his age, he was no longer initiating a damn thing. He'd gotten caught once being the nice guy, and he wasn't falling for that again.

The reality TV show contestant Lexi assumed he'd been with had driven hours from Atlanta to Nashville with a girlfriend to catch his show. Little did he know that she'd used some of her connections with the network to get backstage passes. The TV studio thought it would be a great idea for a meet and greet with country's newest and upcoming star. Photos then showed up all over the internet, making a simple introduction look like a hook-up. He was still resentful about the rumor, mostly because of what it had done to Lexi.

But now that he'd had some time and peace to think, he realized they'd been in trouble before the gossip of infidelity. He'd ignored her from the tour, or taken her for granted like a stupid guy, without even realizing he was doing it. His life had become such a constant schedule of controlled chaos that anything and anyone not right in front of him took a back seat. No one, not even Lexi, had ever taught him how to manage the kind of public life he had to deal with now.

Gary was in touch now daily now, and despite the fact that Luke was supposed to be enjoying some downtime, there were all sorts of requests coming through for his time. Interviews, photo ops, more interviews. He had an interview scheduled with the local channel morning news show tomorrow at four in the morning on Sunday. They were sending a car for him. Beyond that, Luke was stalling. If he said yes to everything he'd no longer have the time and peace to write.

But tonight, he would emerge from his Pepto bottle room, find Lexi, and get her to nail down a time for dinner. Might be pathetic and obvious, but he was going to impress her. He was going to show her she should have never left him. Not now that he'd become everything she deserved. He'd get his second chance or die trying, which, if Lexi had her wish, might happen. She wanted him, which was clear to him every single day, but she didn't *want* to. And Lexi always followed her heart.

The wine tasting hour was hopping tonight, with a

notable lack of couples. Around the fireplace, where someone had started a fire, there were so many younger women gathered, tossing pink and blue hair extensions, and wearing far too few clothes for Monterey Bay weather, that it reminded him of one of his concerts.

"No beer?" He heard a woman wearing a tight-fitting dress ask Lexi.

"Sorry, no. Wine only. We do have water, coffee, and soda."

Dread coursed through him, and he stopped at the entrance to the room. Too late. Everyone in the room had already noticed him. Everyone meaning every single woman. Lips were licked, hair was tossed, and hips were jiggled. He wasn't walking into this room. This room was a trap. He caught Lexi's eye when she turned to see what they'd all stopped to study.

He crooked a finger in her direction. Thankfully, no one else assumed the finger was for them and stayed put.

Lexi, who had been by the cheese and wine display, joined him.

He took her elbow and led her to the adjacent room.

"Yeah?" She turned to him, eyes shimmering in the ambient glow of the fireplace.

"Dinner."

"Right. I said I'd do that."

Funny, she didn't sound happy about it. "When?"

"I don't know."

"That's not an answer. Tomorrow night."

"I'm bus—" She stopped talking when he quirked his eyebrow. "Okay, fine. You sure you don't want to take any of these women to dinner? They seem mighty eager to please."

"No, thanks." He straightened his spine, which today hurt like a bitch after spending too much time in his room hunched over his guitar. "Call me crazy, but I'm a sucker for difficult women whose names end in xi."

She smirked. "I'll see if I can find one for you."

"I've got one, thanks."

"We'll see about that." She turned to go but he caught her wrist.

"Seven o'clock." He nudged his chin towards the women gawking. "Do me a favor. Tell them I'm taken."

She went narrowed eyes on him. "Taken with what?"

"Funny. Tell them I've already got a woman."

"And make it easy for you?" She teased him.

He took another look at the hungry group, and anxiety churned in his gut. At concerts, it was different. There was more of a strict line that wasn't crossed. Here, it was plain weird. He felt like a sideshow freak. The attention wasn't welcome, and not just because Lexi was watching.

"Are they all staying *here*?"

"Well, not all. We're letting a few in at a time for wine tasting since they line up outside waiting to catch a glimpse of you coming or going. But yes. We now have a wait list." She turned in the direction of the women, then back to him. "So…thank you."

He shoved a hand through his hair. "Aw, hell."

"Are you uncomfortable because these women want you, or because I'm here while they want you?"

"All of the above."

"You should be used to it by now."

"I'm not. Never asked for this kind of attention. You know better than anyone that all I ever wanted was to play my guitar."

"Just think of it as a bonus."

He winced. "Do me a favor. Stop messing with me. Yeah?"

"Hmm. Don't think so."

But she smiled when she said it. For the first time since

after he'd kissed her, he thought maybe he might be getting through to her.

LUKE ARRIVED at Lexi's cottage the next evening right on time. He counted three knocks before she finally opened the door for him.

She was still dressed in jeans and a Wilder B&B sweater, her usual work attire. "Oh, that's tonight?"

He braced an arm in the open doorway before she could think about slamming it shut. "You know it is."

She moved aside. "All right then, come in. I'm not quite ready."

Not *quite* ready? She looked as if she hadn't given tonight it any thought at all. But he knew Lexi better, and she wasn't cruel. She was yanking his chain. Having fun teasing him. He stepped inside her small cottage. He'd been here once before and had managed to keep his hands to himself for the most part, even if he'd been inside her bedroom fixing the only bathroom.

The cottage was small enough to have only one bedroom and bathroom. A kitchen and a tiny living area where she had a couch small enough to look like an overstuffed cushion, a TV, and a small bookcase in the corner. It was filled with books and framed photos of her family. Playing music with her sisters on stage. One of Sabrina when she'd made the cover of *Nashville Star*. Oh, and look at that. One of him years ago, standing with the sisters in front of the old tour bus, his arm snaked around Lexi's waist, pulling her in tight.

That man was clearly gobsmacked with love, the expression on his face somewhere between triumph and complete shock. He decided to be encouraged by the fact that she hadn't cut him out of the photo.

Her guitar sat propped near the small couch near the

woodstove. She had a notebook and a pen. She was still writing. Good.

He wanted her to write. Wanted her to remember where she belonged. By his side in the business she should have never left. It would make his plan so much easier. She would come to Nashville with him. He'd marry her and buy her a huge house four of five or ten times the size of this cottage. If she didn't want to go on tour with him, she could come back to Whistle Cove and stay with her sisters when his band went on tour. Once before, Lexi wouldn't rush into marriage, even when they had every reason to get married. And then they'd lost that reason.

He tried not to think about that time. It had been six years ago, and they'd both been too young. Not ready. Things were different now, and he simply wanted tonight to be a new beginning. If she'd allow it.

"Where are we going?" She appeared between French doors that separated the bedroom and living area.

"Someplace nice." He glanced down at his own button-down shirt and black jeans. The ever-present roped friendship bracelets and thick watch on his wrist. Black boots. "But casual."

"I'll be just a minute. Make yourself at home." She headed down the hall, and he heard a door close.

The water went on in the shower, and he realized she was still having her fun with him. Taking a shower and making him wait. And suffer. Note to self: never get on her bad side again. Good thing *The Crow's Nest* didn't take reservations. While he waited, he became familiar with her Netflix watch list, which contained a heavy diet of romantic comedies that didn't surprise him. But they were interspersed with some raunchy stand-up comedians, which did. Leave it to Lexi to be a mystery.

When she emerged from her bedroom, he was in the

middle of watching one of those stand-up routines. One in which a guy was lamenting the fact that his girlfriend didn't like giving him blow jobs. Lexi blushed and looked away. He laughed at the irony. They'd never had any issues in that department. He snapped off the TV with the remote.

"I'm ready." She grabbed a jacket. "Sorry I took so long."

"No problem," he said, determined not to let her rile him or disturb his plans.

Lexi wasn't overly chatty in the sedan, other than asking where they were going every two minutes.

"Why not tell me? It's not a state secret. Are we driving out of town? There are so many restaurants right in Whistle Cove. How far are we driving? Will we be back before midnight?"

It occurred to him that she felt safer asking these questions rather than *talking* to him. She wanted to keep it light and bright, and he'd give her that. For now.

The Crow's Nest was located in Santa Cruz on the shore and next to a marina filled with yachts and speedboats. Impressive ocean views, and more importantly, some of the best New England clam chowder in the area. There was a lounge on the first floor with the occasional band. In fact, the Wilder Sisters had once been regulars here before they had been signed to a record label.

Plenty of memories in this place. They punched into him now, making more than his back ache.

Not only memories of the two of them, but about the part of her life she thought she'd closed the door to. It might be the reason she'd had trouble writing. She was obviously conflicted about the music business. She and her sisters had a love/hate relationship with fame. But she had far more talent than he did, and it was a crime not to share it with the world.

He parked, turned to her, and saw no reaction from Lexi.

She stared at the building. If she was upset he'd brought her here, she didn't show it.

"I haven't been here in…a while." Her voice was low and soft.

He led her inside, hand pressed against the small of her back, and to the top floor where through the floor to ceiling windows they had the best view of the bay. They ordered, and he decided to relax when neither one of them had been recognized.

"You realize the waitress recognized you," Lexi said a moment later.

"She didn't." How had he missed that?

"She did. She's just afraid to say something. Sorry, Luke, but somewhere along the line, you became a sex symbol. Not just a musician."

"That…sucks."

"Sure. Right."

What a shock. She didn't believe him. "Do I *look* like I'm having fun with that kind of attention?"

Because he bet she couldn't answer that honestly, she deflected. "Why do you want two dinner dates with me?"

"We had an agreement."

"Yes, but why?"

"I don't expect anything from you if that's what you're wondering. We're just two old friends out together."

"Well. We were more than friends."

"Exactly. Don't you miss it?" When she quirked her eyebrow, he realized she'd misunderstood him. It was difficult not to laugh. "The *performing*."

"Sometimes." She studied the tablecloth. "I'll remember a particularly good jam or a good night on stage and wish I could recreate it. But we don't get to do that, do we? We can't recreate things that are in the past. Where they belong."

"Maybe we can't recreate, but we can move on. Create new memories."

"That's what I'm trying to do here, Luke." She met his eyes, and he could almost see the wheels spinning.

"Is it working?"

He would add that she didn't look particularly happy *or* satisfied, but maybe he was only seeing what he wanted to see. Wishing for a problem he could fix if it would mean taking her back to Nashville with him. If it could mean a second chance with her.

"It was until *you* got here."

Sorry, not sorry. He kept his mouth shut.

She tapped her fingers on the table. "I guess I'm stuck. But I'll work it out."

"It wasn't all bad."

"No."

"I miss playing with you."

Again, a quirked eyebrow from her. Excuse him, but who in this room (besides him) had the dirty mind? He was going to go ahead and nominate Lexi for this prestigious award.

"*Music.*" He chuckled. "But...all the other stuff, too."

"I don't think we should write any more songs together, in case you were going to ask."

"I wasn't."

"Okay. Because I've already got offers to write with or for Miranda. Her people just want me to send something over first and see how she likes it. I'm thinking this song I wrote might be just the thing."

"Does that mean you'd head to Nashville to work with her?"

His heart kicked up a notch. This might be easier than he'd anticipated. Then again, she was going to Nashville, but that didn't mean she was coming back to him. Still, a step forward.

"I might visit for a week or two. Have some meetings. Then get myself back home."

"Great. Would you stop in and say hi to an old friend?" He slid her a look. Him. He was the *old friend.*

She took a sip of her water and then set the glass down. "Sure, if I have time."

And look at that. A step back.

"Wouldn't want you to go out of your way or anything." There might have been a hint of irritation in his tone. But just a hint.

"Okay."

Aand another step.

They ate mostly in silence for the next few minutes, and when the waitress eventually asked him for an autograph, Luke obliged. Even took a selfie with her.

With their waitress gone, Luke leaned back. "You ever going to stop punishing me for screwing up?"

Her eyes widened. She put her soup spoon down, blotted her lips with the napkin, and put it back in her lap. "I'm not—"

"Yes. You are."

"Okay." She sighed. "I'll stop now."

"Would be nice. You said you don't hate me."

"And I don't."

"Maybe not. But you sure hate to *like* me."

She blinked. "I don't even know what that means."

They finished eating. He paid, giving the waitress slash fan a generous tip. As they were walking out they heard music wafting through the building.

"Let's go in and support a local artist," he said.

"Sure."

He took her hand and led her to a table in the back. Never let it be said he wanted to steal the show from a hard-working musician. The guitar player was a solo act, and he was relying on a steady stream of covers of chart topping hits and the occasional request. It's the way most musicians started out, including the infamous Wilder Sisters. No one wanted to hear originals until they were played on the radio first.

Someone in the audience requested *Stairway to Heaven*, and the dude segued into that right after a cover of *Friends in Low Places*. Guy was versatile, Luke would say that for him.

He turned to smile at Lexi, but she'd caught the attention of the waitress.

"Two Coronas." She held up her fingers. "And this is Luke Wyatt, by the way. Might want to tell your performer. Maybe he'll come up and sing one for the crowd."

Luke froze. The waitress nodded, smiled in his direction, and left to get their drinks.

"What did you do that for?" Luke said.

"You didn't come in here to perform?"

"Damn it, Lexi. No, I *didn't*."

"But you won't mind."

Time to call her out on all the crap she'd been slinging his way. "Not if *you* don't."

"W-what?"

"You heard me. C'mon, girl. We have our chart-topping hit to perform. I've been playing it for a year all over the country. Now it's your damned turn."

CHAPTER 10

"Batshit crazy really brings out the color in my eyes." ~ Meme

Lexi's knees had turned to rubber. Two useless pieces of latex which couldn't be counted on right now to do the tough, but necessary, work of holding her upright. Of steering her to the stage where Luke already waited. His lips tipped up in a smile, but his eyes were dark and challenging. She'd pushed and pushed, and now he was finally furious. Now she'd really done it. She should have quit while she was ahead, and oh she was ahead by her count. Sure, Luke had embarrassed her a little bit by finding her raunchy comedy shows. They were funny. She couldn't help that.

Now he'd taken her to dinner in a place so full of memories, her heart hurt.

She'd talked to him for the first time after a show in this very place. A lanky man-boy with iridescent brown eyes, twenty years old, and full of piss and fire. He'd said one word to her (hey) and made her palms sweaty and her heart skip a beat or two. She'd nearly fainted because she didn't talk to boys. Didn't know how.

She'd been so busy with school, performing, and band practice, that she'd never met many boys. Certainly not ones with dark eyes that glittered, framed by long dark lashes. Her eighteen-year-old self thought the sensation worse than stage fright. All the confusing emotions of desire and lust mixed with the panic that he'd brought to the surface had been foreign to her. Butterflies in her stomach weren't a good analogy. Butterflies were small. How about a herd of elephants?

Tonight, she'd made him wait, teasing him while she took a shower and her sweet time. She'd dressed in a blue sweater with a drop in the back, tight jeans, and kickass boots. She'd told him she couldn't care less if she ever saw him in Nashville, while the truth was that it would be nice to have someone to hang out with.

She couldn't seem to help herself, because the hotter he looked, the meaner she got. It seemed to be the only way to refrain from ripping off his clothes and knocking boots. She wasn't ready to go there with him, so she had to stop him from coming at her like a freight train on crack. She was a different woman now than the girl he'd met. One who understood that some men in the music business took what they wanted. Used people.

"...songwriting partner, Lexi Wilder," Luke finished introducing her.

Because she'd been trained to do so since she was a teenager, even on days when she had a pimple and a raging case of PMS, Lexi strode up the stage and accepted the guitar someone handed her. And it all came back to her like rusty pipes forced to push water through again. Like an old sun-bleached garden hose laid out in the backyard for years.

"How are you all doing tonight? Some of you here tonight might remember, but my sisters and I started playing here a few years back." She strummed her guitar. "It's such a pleasure to be here tonight with Mr. Luke Wyatt."

Applause from the audience.

"Pleasure's all mine, Lexi." Luke played a chord progression and winked at her. "Should we take requests?"

Smooth Luke.

"Falling for Forever!" called someone from the audience. They all clapped.

A look passed between her and Luke. In that passing glance, she saw a flash of pain in his brown eyes, filtered through the professional smile he'd pasted on his face. Lexi swallowed the golf ball in her throat. The last time she'd played this song had been with Luke shortly after they'd written it. She hadn't either played or heard the song in months, but had a feeling she could remember every word, seeing as they'd all come from her heart.

Luke didn't hesitate. He merely nodded, smiled, and played the chord progression through once. She saw it as the bone he'd thrown her way, so she'd be able to catch on if she'd forgotten. As if she ever would. Following his lead, she played her guitar and listened to Luke sing the words. Words written by a lovesick woman. Tender words.

I never thought I'd fall...But now I see a promise in your eyes... falling for forever...

When Luke began the chorus, he moved his body and guitar, angling towards her. She knew what he wanted. He wanted her to join in with the harmony, as she'd done before. She obliged. Her soft alto voice was a perfect blend with his baritone. His voice was deep and rich, like chocolate mixed with espresso. She'd always thought hers to be too light and airy, like cotton candy, and about as sweet as ribbon candy. It was the reason Sabrina had become their lead singer, because her soprano voice was strong and powerful. Lusty. Just like Sabrina. But Lexi had a skill Sabrina didn't. She could always find the perfect third harmony by instinct, which made her able to blend well with almost anyone. One of the benefits of having first been a keyboard player.

Somehow, she got through the song, the words imprinted on her brain. Then again, it helped that she hadn't written a love song since. Maybe the time had come to write another one, so *that song* could take a back seat. Fade to black. She could finally move forward and not just pretend. Because that's what she'd been doing for a year. Standing stock still. Believing that music was just something she'd once done for a living, might someday do again to make some money, and not who she was at heart.

Nothing could be further from the truth.

AFTER THEY'D PERFORMED a few more songs for the audience and left *Crow's Nest*, Lexi didn't even wait until she got to the car. "Why did you do that to me?"

He stopped midway to the passenger side. "You deserved it, baby." There was a clipped and angry edge to his voice.

She pulled on the handle of the door, hoping he'd catch the hint and unlock it. "I did not. I tried to do a nice thing for you and you blindsided me."

When he reached her side, he made no move to click the lock but instead his hand gripped the nape of her neck and pulled her to him. His long fingers dove into her hair, roaming, clutching. The sensation of his warm hand in her hair felt electric and far better than it should.

Not particularly gently, he tilted her head up to meet his blazing eyes. "You tried to embarrass me."

"No."

"You can't lie to me. Remember that. Want to try again?" Luke said.

"Do you know I haven't even listened to the radio in months? I don't want to hear *Falling for Forever* ever again. I hate that song! And you made me play and sing it in front of a bunch of strangers."

Tears threatened to spill from her eyes and she bit her lower lip so she could hurt for an entirely different reason. Not because one song had that much power over her.

"Want to know what it's been like for me? Singing it every night and sometimes twice. Probably think it doesn't matter to me, don't you?" His fingers, tangled in her hair, tugged a little tighter. "My moneymaker, so I should just shut up and sing."

She refused to be intimidated. "Well, if the chorus fits...and I saw you on award show night, looking pretty damned happy singing our song."

"Glad you're calling it what it is. *Our* song."

His fingers disentangled from her hair and lowered to her lips. The movement felt so possessive, the sensation of his long fingers tracing the outline of her lips, so familiar that her bones ached.

Exhaustion shadowed his eyes, and there was strain in his broad shoulders. "We've been through hell together, Lexi. Don't let it end now."

"You were the one who gave up first." Pain pierced through her all over again.

"It takes two, baby. You gave up on us. Admit it."

"I gave up on the road. *Not* you." She drilled a finger into his chest.

Life on the road had simply cost her too much over the years. Moving from one city to another, yet never seeing much but the inside of a bus or hotel room. Though she'd been invited to be part of Luke's backup band by the label, it had felt like a slap in the face after years of hard work. After years of punishing tours. It also felt like a betrayal to her sisters.

Luke had claimed he'd wanted her along, whether as part of the band or not. In the end, she'd turned the gig down, and told Luke she'd come out and see him perform every chance she had. She told herself, too, that he deserved this chance to be the front man. A star. He deserved his time to shine. Luke had been in the background of everything from the moment he'd been born. This would be his chance, and she'd wanted that for him.

She'd wanted it up until the moment she saw him smiling and laughing with other women. Until the moment her own insecurities rose from the pile of rubble that had been her career. Maybe their closeness had been due to proximity on a tour bus for years when they only had each other. He'd been grateful for the chance to play his guitar and make a living, but maybe he'd simply used both her and her family.

She didn't want to believe it, but ever since they'd been apart, it was a shadow behind her that never went away.

Luke's eyes softened, and his hand tipped up her chin. "For the record, baby, I never gave up on you."

He finally brought his hand down and used it to unclick the lock, open the passenger door, and wait for Lexi to climb in. During all of it, he never once broke eye contact.

On the quiet drive back, Lexi reflected on the evening. Thanks to Luke, she'd come to realize that music would have to somehow fit into a part of her life again. It wasn't just what she did for a living, it was who she was. Even if he'd done so by forcing the issue, which she wasn't crazy about, he'd done her a favor.

"Okay. Look, I'm sorry."

He simply stared out the windshield into the now dark

night, jaw tight, he kept driving and gave her no clue to his thoughts.

"I've been horrible to you. And I didn't mean to suggest that you wanted to take away the spotlight tonight. I've been picking on you and prodding you, hoping to push you away. For crying out loud, *why* don't you hate me? Why don't you give up on me?"

He threw her a sideways glance. "Think about that for a minute."

She thought about it for a grand total of three seconds. "Because you're a sucker for punishment."

"Not at all, honey, but I'm a sucker for the woman sitting next to me. That might be true." He reached for her hand, threading his fingers through hers. "I won't give up because you never gave up on me. When Reggie kicked me out and I didn't have a place to stay, you had your dad find me a place. When I showed up late to practices in those first years, you begged your dad to give me another chance. And another. I thought I'd lost everything until I met you. There were times I didn't treat you right. But you always let me back in. You loved me when I was nobody."

It felt unbelievably good to hear those words coming from him. She studied their hands together, his long lean fingers tangled with her smaller ones. She'd always loved his hands for what they could do with a guitar. Envied him. There was ease there, a rock-hard confidence that came from being so familiar with the instrument. Comfortable. Unlike Lexi, the guitar had been his first and only instrument. Unlike Lexi, who'd started to perform mostly out of family duty and obligation, Luke did so because he loved to play.

He squeezed her fingers. "In case you didn't know, I'm crazy about you."

Her heart swelled up like a balloon in her chest, far too

big to fit. She felt her eyes water, bit her lower lip, and tried not to cry. "Luke—"

"I know. You don't have to say anything. I'm just telling you how I feel. I don't expect anything from you at all."

"Nothing?"

"Well, it would be nice if you at least liked me again." He made a turn into the B&B and let go of her hand. "Oh, yeah. And one more thing."

She laughed. "Just *one* more thing?"

He parked close to her cottage and shut off the car. "Forget about the song. I want you to tell me what it felt like up there tonight. You and me playing together."

She squirmed in her seat and unbuckled her seat belt. "I enjoyed myself, mostly."

Liar. It was awesome. Like coming home. Especially singing with Luke. Their voices were a perfect blend.

He grinned, the smile spreading to the small crinkles around his sharp, intelligent eyes. "You're a natural. And you looked happy."

"I was trained to do it." She lifted a shoulder. "It's odd. I always thought of Sabrina as the singer because she's so much better than me. She's a performer. But I do like singing, as long as it's not by myself."

"You're a great singer, too. No one can harmonize like you do."

He walked her to the door of her cottage. It was such a quiet night, she only heard the sound of the crashing waves. The sounds of seagulls in the distance. A perfect night. A night for lovers, and she would walk into her cottage alone. Just as she'd done for the past year. She'd told herself she didn't want to start a relationship until she got her head straight. Until she figured out the rest of her life. Now, an uncomfortable sensation tightened her stomach. Maybe she'd been waiting for Luke to come for her all along.

Waiting for him to come and fight for her. Waiting for her first love.

"You kept up your end of the deal and went to dinner with me," he said.

Did he seriously think she wouldn't? A deal was a deal.

"We still have one more dinner date." She found her keys in the bottom of her purse.

Her hand shook visibly when she brought it to the keyhole and unlocked the door. Why was she talking about the next date? If she hadn't mentioned it like a love-sick woman, he might forget about it. If he'd just give up on her and go away, this would all be so much easier. She'd go back to her regularly scheduled programming, trying to figure out the rest of her life.

One thing she did know about Luke was that he never gave up. He wouldn't have even survived his life without putting up a hell of a fight. Now she was faced with the fact she was extremely drawn to a man she had no business being with. She didn't want his life anymore, and he would never give up what he had now for her, nor would she ask him to.

"Next date's your choice. Tomorrow night." He stood in the now open doorway, arms braced against the frame.

"Tomorrow? That's soon."

"Yeah, and?"

"I thought maybe we could wait a few days."

"Why? You busy?"

Not anymore than normal, but after tonight, she might need a break from the force of nature that was Luke Wyatt. It had become difficult to forget the way he kissed. The way he held her like he had claimed her a long time ago.

"Not really, but—"

"Good. Tomorrow, then." He turned to go but she stopped him.

"Okay, but I want to go to the boardwalk."

"The *boardwalk?*"

Right now, he was probably thinking that wasn't much of a place for a date, at least not for locals who were over eighteen. She nodded.

"The boardwalk it is, baby."

And then he turned and walked away.

CHAPTER 11

"You can't control everything. Your hair was put on your head to remind you of that." ~ Meme

The next morning, Lexi had just finished restocking the towels in one of their rooms when she noticed a peculiar looking woman standing on the outside walkway in a big floppy hat, wearing a Hawaiian Mumu style dress that seemed to swallow her small figure. She looked vaguely familiar.

Lexi did a double-take. "Sabrina?"

She turned, and Lexi took in the black wig that completed the disguise. She hadn't seen that one in a while.

"How did you know it was me?"

"Um, I'm your sister?" Lexi deadpanned.

"But you don't think anyone else would recognize me, right?"

"It's not likely."

"Good."

They walked together towards the main lodge. "What's

up?" Lexi asked. "Anyone come around here giving you a hard time?"

"Not yet, but with Luke here, and that photographer around, I can never be too careful. I got tired of hiding in my room."

That bothered Lexi more than it probably did Sabrina. She had Luke to thank for bringing the Wilder Sisters a renewal in attention, but she also had to thank him for zero vacancy and a long wait list. Catch-22.

"You shouldn't have to hide."

The daily news cycle brought a scandal every day. Of course, most of the people of Whistle Cove didn't much care about scandals that were far worse than Sabrina's indiscretion. They simply cared that this was Sabrina *Wilder*, one of their own, and she should have known better.

Outsiders, however, had been far less forgiving. The emails and tweets had said so.

"I know, but hey, sometimes it's kind of fun. And I put together these outfits, so might as well get some more use out of them."

When Lexi thought back to over a year ago, life in Whistle Cove was much better now. On the road, they'd been hounded after The Scandal. Tabloid magazines had begged for an interview, and when refused, pieced together what they could from "confidential sources." Paparazzi hounded them from city to city on the last leg of their tour, hoping to catch a glimpse of the terrible, awful, no good, reckless Sabrina Wilder. The record label wouldn't have minded much if all of that had helped sales. Unfortunately, it had the opposite effect. At home, they'd endured some chastising for a short while from some of the less than kind townspeople.

"You need to stop worrying what people think. If they want to slut shame you, that's their problem. They don't know you."

"How did it go with Luke yesterday?" Sabrina changed the subject.

"All right. Except he took me to the *Crow's Nest*. Forced me to get up and sing *the song*."

Even under the shadow caused by the wide brimmed hat, Lexi got a good look at Sabrina's wide eyes. "Really? You got up and played?"

"I tried to set him up, and he set *me* up."

"I don't know why you won't give him another chance. It's not like *he'd* ever sell photos of your boobs to the highest bidder."

Sure, and that was Lexi's only requirement for a man. "I'd never *send* him photos of my boobs."

"Right, why would you? He can see them anytime he wants."

Lexi shook her head. "Not anymore."

A few guests walked past them on their way to the beach, and smiles and nods were exchanged.

Sabrina suddenly stopped and put her hand on Lexi's shoulder. "You don't have to stay away from music because of me. You still have a chance at a career."

"That's true of you too. But I'm not interested in life on the road again."

"Yeah, that stuff got old real fast."

"I'm just going to try and write songs, and that's it. No need to perform with Luke or anyone else."

Although, she'd missed it. A little. It was nice being on stage with Luke. Except for having to sing their song, she'd enjoyed it. It hadn't been as terrible as she'd imagined. She'd strummed the guitar, and everything had come back to her. But the life-style of a working musician was unhealthy, and she'd paid too high a price for that once. She wanted a balanced life. A chance at a family again someday. With a good man.

"But Luke's a good man," Sabrina said, and Lexi wondered if she'd said that last part out loud.

"For someone." Lexi grinned.

"Damn, you're so stubborn."

"So are you. Okay, so your squeaky-clean image is gone, but you can re-invent yourself. Do you ever think about performing again?"

"Sometimes. Sure. Guess it's in my blood."

And even now, Sabrina was performing. The disguises and outfits. They were fun for her, a chance to be someone else.

"I might miss wine tasting tonight. I need you to help Jessie, make sure we have enough wine for the crowd we have now. We might have to pull some from the cellar."

"Where are you going?"

"I have one more date with Luke. It was part of our deal. I chose the boardwalk. Figure it would be too hard to get romantic there. Lots of families and kids everywhere. Plus, I have a craving for a waffle cone."

"Remind me never to get on your bad side."

"Girl, you've been on my bad side since the moment you were born."

"Ha, ha." Sabrina shoulder checked Lexi.

They parted at the entrance to the lodge, where Sabrina went one way and Lexi went the other. She could see that the lodge was already filled with women as had become the norm. Sabrina breezed by them, unidentified, but a few of the ladies threw curious glances in her direction. This time Lexi guessed it was more for the over the top outfit than anything else.

Lexi had wanted to go to dinner early enough that they'd run into all the families out on a weekend. Most who visited the boardwalk were from all over the Bay Area, and places like San Jose, Palo Alto, and Gilroy. Lexi hadn't been there in years and it would be a nice throwback.

As the afternoon wore on, and she hadn't heard from Luke, she went looking for him. He wasn't going to get her to the boardwalk after dark, when the place was winding down and grown-ups were cuddled on the beach around small bonfires. She didn't want to cuddle. Didn't want him kissing her again. That one time of weakness had been bad enough. She'd need to do better with her Luke Shield.

She knocked on the door to his room, where he seemed to mostly hide these days, but he didn't answer. He was in there, and she could hear him, but he wouldn't come to the door. Was he with a woman?

Whipping out the phone she'd just started carrying around again, she texted him:

Open the door. I know you're in there.

L.W.: Can't. I'm naked.

What's her name?

L.W.: Give me a break.

She was teasing him again because she didn't honestly believe there was anyone else in there. That wasn't the Luke she knew and loved. She understood that now and that her jealousy had probably flared too high, though she doubted it was entirely her fault. She waited a few more seconds for his response, staring at her phone. When it didn't come, she figured he'd given her an out for today. And she would take it because just being near him had started to mess with her resolve.

She could sleep with him, sure she could. And then what? What happened when he left for Nashville and that world that currently made her want to break out in hives?

The door slammed open, and there stood a shirtless Luke wearing nothing but jeans with the top two buttons still undone. His shoulders were still damp. His hair was wet as if he'd just hopped out of the shower. He held the door wide open, too, like he wanted her to see he was indeed alone.

She barely resisted the urge to face palm because her playful attitude had had the reverse effect and instead held up her hand to study her fingernails. Better than staring at his abs.

"Oh, okay. Um…"

He folded his arms across his broad chest. "Flattering."

"What?"

"Your opinion of me. That I would have a girl in here when I have a dinner date with you tonight."

"Luke, you used to know when I was teasing you. Listen, I just wanted to tell you I'd like our date today to be early."

"Early at the Boardwalk's going to be a lot of kids. Families." He quirked a brow. "Our deal was for dinner."

"Right. But I'll need an early dinner. I'm…tired."

She expected him to argue, but he simply quirked a brow, then nodded. "Might as well. Got to do a morning show tomorrow anyway. They're sending a car at four in the freaking morning."

"They're having you work while you're here?"

"Why not?" He shrugged. "Spending a lot of time in my room."

She caught sight of empty pizza boxes on the table. Soda cans on the nightstand. He was definitely living like a bachelor. "You know we have maid service if you request it."

"Nah. I'll do it."

"Are you still writing?"

If he was writing his own songs again, then he surely wouldn't need her. She'd trust him a little more if she could believe he wasn't at all interested in her pursuing music again simply because he wanted another hit like their first one. But no. That wasn't Luke. He'd given her no indication that he was here for any other reason than her.

"Six so far. It's been like two a day. Crazy."

"I'm happy for you."

He rubbed at the stubble on his chin. "Being home has been good for me. Reminded me of where I came from, and who I am."

"And that's Maggie Wyatt's son."

His eyes shimmered like they did every time he heard his beautiful mother's name. No one in Whistle Cove talked about her anymore. It was easier that way.

"Thanks for that, baby."

"I'll see you at four." She turned on her heel and left.

* * *

FOUR O'CLOCK ROLLED AROUND, and Luke emerged from the safety of his room to find Lexi. He was still affected by the mention of his mother. Lexi had been the only person he would talk to as he prepared for his trial testimony. Now the memory was tender and raw because of the one other instance in which he'd failed to protect and keep someone he loved. But he'd been younger, most kind people reminded him, and no match for Reggie.

Tonight was his last chance to get back the second woman he'd ever loved.

He'd never cheated on Lexi, but long separations had chipped away at trust, and it never helped when the media wanted to create a story that just wasn't there.

Lexi didn't need to perform if she didn't want to, but she had to be by his side. He should have exercised his domineering ways at the moment most required. Should have fought like hell for her, so there would be no question in her mind that he needed her, but instead he'd caved and let her go. He'd believed it was what she'd wanted and needed. Time away from the stress of the road. Time to recuperate from the gossip with her sisters. And he'd been trying to fit into the new, carefully crafted image they'd created for him. And that wasn't a caveman who would throw his woman over his shoulder.

But he wouldn't be making that mistake again. This time, he wouldn't be leaving Whistle Cove without his woman. Even if that made him sound like a caveman. Ask him how much he cared.

Once they'd arrived at the boardwalk, which was the usual tourist trap, Lexi wanted to stroll the gift shops. His least favorite thing to do was waiting while she *shopped*. Also known as walking down every aisle, picking up a blouse, sweater, or other trinket, staring at the price tag, scowling, and putting it back. He wanted to buy the sterling silver necklace and earrings set she studied for a while before putting it down without a frown, but knew how well she'd take that, so didn't even try.

He put up with four of these specialty shops until a young clerk said, "Hey, aren't you—?"

"Nope," Luke said, took Lexi's hand, and hauled her out of the shop.

"Luke, I wasn't—"

"Enough." He tugged her away from the shops. "You're not going to buy anything. Never do."

"But I—"

"This is my time, remember? You agreed."

"I didn't agree for you to interfere with my shopping."

"Not doing that," he said, though he most certainly was. Screw it. "I'm hungry."

"You're always hungry."

"Maybe, but this is a dinner date. We need to get to the food portion for it to actually be dinner."

She folded arms across her chest. "I want hot dogs."

"I think I can spring for a bigger dinner than that, baby."

"That's what I want."

She sounded like a crabby child now, one he should take over his knee. "Why not."

Big spender that he was, he sprang for four hot dogs, fries, and soft drinks. They carried them down the steps to the beach, found a place to sit on the sand, and ate mostly in silence. One taste of the beef hot dog, and he had to agree that Lexi was right. Just because he now had loads of money, it didn't mean he couldn't still appreciate the little things. Bigger things too, like the ocean waves crashing before him, making their own unique kind of music. He'd always lived near the ocean and didn't know how well he'd fare in Nashville long-term. Maybe he'd make Whistle Cove home base again once he got to call the shots.

He glanced at her sitting next to him, the wind whipping her wild blonde hair all around her, her fighting it back as she always did. Force of habit had him tucking a big strand behind her ear. Just then a group of kids ran past them, kicking up sand on their way to the waves. A couple walked by, each holding on to the hand of a toddler.

"Lots of families here," he said. Made it difficult to get romantic, especially for them, which had likely been her plan all along.

"Yep."

Lexi got the fathomless and pained look in her eyes that she did every time she saw young children, and he wondered if she'd done this to punish him in another way. The idea kicked him in the gut like it did every single time, until he pushed the feelings back down along with all the other unpleasant memories from his past. There were boatloads of those, from watching his beautiful but weak mother take a daily beating for years, to the year he'd finally lost her, and suddenly become homeless and hungry. Aimless. He'd done some stuff he wasn't proud of to stay alive and breathing because he was nothing if not a survivor.

They finished eating, and he gathered their trash. "Want something else, baby?"

"What?" She glanced at him as if she'd forgotten he sat right next to her.

"Did I lose you?"

"I'm right here." She pressed her lips together and shoved all her wild hair back with both hands.

"Yeah, right." He stood. "Do you want something else to eat?"

She looked up at him. "I would love a waffle cone."

"Got it. Wouldn't mind one myself. Be right back."

This is what a date at the boardwalk meant, after all. Eating lousy junk food for the day, and remembering what it was like to be a kid.

He climbed up the concrete steps and made his way to the waffle cones.

CHAPTER 12

"If Cinderella's shoe fit so perfectly, then why did it fall off?"~ Meme

While she waited on the beach for Luke and a waffle cone, Lexi got caught up in a daydream, remembering what it had been like to come here with her sisters years ago. Cotton candy, hot dogs, bumper cars. The roller coaster. Way before daddy had figured out that Sabrina was a born performer, Lexi was a natural at making up songs out of the blue, and Jessie would do whatever she'd been asked to do. The band had been formed shortly after Lexi started seventh grade, and after that, there hadn't been much time to do fun kid stuff anymore. Daddy had loved his daughters, sure, but he certainly worked them. Mom had enjoyed making their matching outfits, and doing their hair and make-up. Make-up, even for ten-year-old Sabrina.

Lexi hadn't known it was weird or strange until some of her friends made comments. She'd been forced to defend her parents and her sister, who happened to love the make-up, even if it was a little obscene. Still, for years they'd been the picture of an all-American family. Sisters singing clean and wholesome songs and traveling together. The outfits were always matching and always modest. She'd say that for her parents. They hadn't wanted to make sex symbols out of their young daughters.

Long ago, she'd decided that it would be different once she had a child. Were she ever privileged to bring a child into this world she'd guard the child's life like a bank guarded its vault. She'd discourage a career in the music industry, but once they were adults, she certainly couldn't stop them. But a child deserved a childhood. They deserved a life without complications. Without worrying about dwindling record sales, selling tickets to appearances, and most of all, having enough money. They'd have their entire adult lives to worry about that. She intended to take care of her children so they would never be brought into adult conversations and decisions.

"Danny!" A woman shouted as she went through the crowd. "Danny!"

She stopped next to Lexi, who glanced up at a woman wearing a wide-brimmed hat and a one-piece swimsuit.

"Have you seen a little boy about this high?" She held out her arm. "His brother was supposed to be watching him, and he came back without him. Danny!"

She went on screaming, a wrecked expression in her eyes, the terror in her voice evident with each passing second. "He's five. Five-years-old. Danny!"

"I'll help you look."

Because of cut backs, lifeguards were in limited supply, which meant that everyone swam at their own risk.

That doesn't mean he's in the water. He could be anywhere. Kids liked games, and there was an entire arcade behind them. Maybe he'd taken off there. Yes, yes. That was it. It doesn't mean he's in the water. Lexi repeated this over and over, running like a tape in her brain, a way to calm her mind from jumping to conclusions. She stood and was about to ask her for a description when her eye caught something blue bopping in the waves. She thought for a second that she saw an arm reach out.

Oh, God, no. Lexi didn't want to believe it, but it could be the woman's son. A child in the water, drowning. There was no time to get help, and no time to tell his mother, who had moved on, shouting his name with ever-increasing panic. Without a second thought, Lexi tore through the sunbathers and those who stayed at the edge, letting only the waves touch their feet.

"Out of my way!" She threw off her shoes, crested a wave, and dove into the cold waters of the bay.

The ocean on the central coast wasn't California-warm like some tourists expected. It wasn't Los Angeles or San Diego, where the gulf brought warmer temperatures that meant a reasonable swim by reasonable people. Here, anyone other than children, usually took to the water in a wet suit. Whether the sun was shining after the fog bank rolled back or not, the water stayed near arctic temperatures and perfect for sharks.

Lexi stopped thinking as she swam toward the child, who she could clearly now see in her sights thrashing about in the water. She wasn't the greatest swimmer, and now struggled against a powerful wave. She came up from under its tow and found the boy, somehow finding the strength somehow to grab him and pull him up. He was limp in her arms, which terrified her, but might make it easier to drag him back to shore. Her arm wrapped around his waist, she took a big breath, dove under, and heaved him up.

When she came back up, and before Lexi could even turn to make her way back, she felt strong arms dragging her.

Luke. Good, he was a far better swimmer than she'd ever be. She held on fiercely to the child with both arms now while Luke dragged them back.

Once at the shore, they were surrounded by a crowd of onlookers and Danny's mother.

"An ambulance is on the way," someone said. "We've notified beach security."

Lexi could only stare at the scene before her and shake from both the cold and fear. Danny's mother was useless. She was screaming, turning in circles, hands on top of her hat as if she couldn't believe this was happening. But Luke rolled the child on his side, lifting his arms above his head. Bending to listen to his chest, he began mouth to mouth. He did so until beach security arrived. Two seconds after they arrived, Danny coughed, sputtered up water and began crying for his mother.

The most beautiful sound in the world.

Thank God. Her heart was slamming against her chest, but she felt a strange sense of power, too. Shivering, Lexi took in the scene. Two waffle cones were thrown in the sand. She watched as Luke walked to them, picked them up, and threw them in a trash can. Walk was not the right word. Stalked was more like it. He wasn't happy to be wet and shivering. He could join her club.

"I'm sorry," she said through her haze even though she wasn't a bit sorry. They'd done the right thing.

"Let's go." He took her hand and tugged her up to him. "You need to get out of those wet clothes."

All the way to the car, he wouldn't speak to her. Once they were driving, and he'd turned the heater on to relieve some of her shaking, she spoke. "I ruined our date, but nothing was more important. I'm sorry you're mad, but we'll get dry again. I'll pay for the waffle cones."

"*That's* why you think I'm pissed?" A tick formed in his jaw as he spoke.

"Isn't it?"

"We'll talk about this later."

Later. It was always later with Luke when it came to emotionally wrenching topics. He could put his pain into songs, but he wouldn't *talk* to her. He pulled in beside her cottage and followed her to the front door. No sooner had she put the key in than he opened the door, let himself in after her, and shut it behind them.

"Luke, I don't—"

"Get these wet clothes off." He wrenched his own drenched shirt off, and when she didn't move fast enough he pulled hers off.

"Hey!"

"I'm not playing around here, baby. It's nothing I haven't seen before. You need to get naked. Now. Don't know if you realize it, but you're close to being a shade of blue. Had half a mind to send you on the ambulance, too. The car heater didn't help much considering those clothes have been in the bay."

He was right about that. She was still shivering. And he was taking off more of his clothes, as if they had never been apart a day, much less one year. Jeans, socks, boxers.

Boxers!

She blinked. "Luke—"

He glanced at her. "Why are you still dressed? Don't make me do it because you know I will."

Knowing that to be one hundred percent true, she hurriedly pulled off her jeans, having a little trouble sliding them off her hips until he helped tug them off her. She glared at him and slapped his hand away, which only made him grin. Then she stepped and turned away from him to take care of the bra and panties.

"Hit the shower," he said. "Get warm."

She ran to the bathroom, turned on the showerhead, reached for and threw him a towel. The last thing she needed right now was to see him completely naked for another second.

"Thanks," he said before she shut the door to him and all his virile manly nakedness.

She could handle a dip in the bay with her clothes on. She could handle trying to save a drowning child, but right now she couldn't take Luke Wyatt naked. At the moment, she was trying to decide whether to tell him she still had a pair of his old, gray sweat pants. She'd worn them so often to bed, they'd somehow become hers, though they were way too long for her. Now, she kept them in her bottom dresser drawer and hadn't worn them in months.

Tell Luke she still had his old sweats, or put up with him in a towel for however much longer he would be here?

The warm water pounded her skin, thawing her body as well as her mind. What had she been thinking going in after the boy when there were other people who could have helped? The thought that it might not have been just one person drowning, but two, hadn't occurred to her. Until now. Yet it was the first line of defense in any rescue scenario. First take care of yourself because you can't help anyone else if you're useless. Geez, she was such a dummy. She couldn't explain what had taken her over and made her act before thinking except for the piercing knowledge that she didn't want Danny's mother to suffer such a huge loss.

That kind of pain never quite went away.

She dried herself off and bundled into the fuzzy white bathrobe hanging on a hook on the back of her bathroom door. As she opened the door, the waft of steam followed her out, and she hoped Luke was taking advantage of that towel. She found him sitting in front of her black kettle furnace. His back to her, he didn't turn, which gave her time to examine that beautiful back. It was all hard planes and solid, brawny angles. A working man's back, because Luke had been that for most of his life.

He finally turned to her. "You okay?"

"I'm better. Thank you. You were right. I was freezing. Anyway, I'm good now, so you can go."

"Not going anywhere." He turned back to the heat of the kettle.

"What?"

"I said I'm not going."

"Really, Luke? You're going to pick an argument with me now? You took care of me, I get it. Thank you very much, and now you can go!"

"I can't. First, I'll definitely attract too much attention going to my room dressed only in a towel. Second, we're not done here."

She could ask one of her sisters to get him some clothes from his room, but that would invite a ton of questions. Eventually, she'd tell them everything, of course, because that's what she did. Just not now.

"What do you mean we're not done here?"

"I said we'd talk about it later. Now it's later."

"It is?" She couldn't recall a time when Luke hadn't stalled on 'later.' Hadn't kissed her until she forgot they were supposed to 'talk.'

"Yeah, baby."

"What if I don't want to talk about it?"

He snorted. "You will."

"I don't have anything much to say."

"Yeah?"

"Yeah." She crossed her arms.

He stood, took two steps towards her, and she worried with each step that the towel would slip. But it seemed to be sewn on to his lower half. "Want to know why I was so pissed?"

"Why?"

"When I saw you in that water, the only thing I could think of was what if I lost you? What if you and the kid both drowned? Know how often that's happened? You're not the greatest swimmer, babe, and you should have waited for me."

"I know I should have but—"

"I know exactly why you didn't wait. Just don't ever do it again." He reached to take hold of her chin and tip it up. "Ever."

"I don't like it when you tell me what to do." She spit out the words.

"Tough." He was smiling, a man without a clue he was about to get slapped.

Instead of slapping him she took a deep breath, stalked over to her dresser drawer and found the pair of sweat pants. Threw them at him, and he caught them in the air. "Forgot I have these."

"Thanks, baby." He dropped the towel, not even bothering to turn around, and slipped the pants on.

Since he wouldn't turn away, she did, giving him her back, fuming at the familiarity with which he treated this occasion. While busy fuming, she suddenly found herself catching air as he gathered her in his arms and started walking to her bedroom. Oh, hell no. It wasn't going to be this easy.

"What are you *doing*?"

"Putting you in bed." He set her down. "Under the covers."

"What?"

"Under the covers, I said. You still feel cold to me. That sea water gets deep down in your skin, and it takes hours to warm up."

He ought to know. Luke used to work the boats by the

wharf with his dad before...before everything. She would get outraged again, but he actually drew the covers back for her and then tucked her in. Which meant he was obviously not thinking they were going to have sex. And, oh he was so right about that.

She lay under the covers wondering when Luke got so compassionate, then remembered a time when he'd taken care of her. After the baby. Especially then.

Five years ago, when she'd missed her period, Lexi hadn't panicked. She hadn't been exactly regular. But then an entire month passed. Busy on the road with performing and touring, she'd neglected to notice the passage of time. The over-the-counter test Luke picked up for her had been positive. They were both terrified and cautiously happy. But they were also in the middle of a 24-city tour with contractual obligations. Luke wanted to get married immediately but Lexi didn't want to get married just because she was pregnant. Of course, her parents wouldn't have loved *that* news.

She didn't tell anyone except her sisters and prepared to break the news to her parents, who weren't on the tour bus with them. They had planned to meet in Texas on their way back to California. It wasn't going to be an easy conversation, and she had not looked forward to it. She was part of the *Wilder* family, but the family name had been a bit of a joke. Her great-great-grandfather had years ago changed the family name to Wilder from Wilzenski, which didn't have as nice of a ring to it. But Dad had taken pride in the fact that his daughters were the opposite of wild.

Lexi had been about to prove to him that she'd messed up by falling in love. Now, she would have a baby. She hadn't been a bit sorry. Still, she planned to break the news gently. She'd finish out her contractual obligations but after that, she'd need a time-out from the touring. Sabrina and Jessie understood. They needed a break, too. It wasn't healthy to be on a tour bus for months on end. She'd need easy access to fresh fruit, healthy meals, and regular medical care.

But Lexi never had a chance to tell her parents because she lost the pregnancy somewhere between Austin and Houston.

She didn't think about the baby all that often anymore.

"Lexi."

It seemed she was crying. How had she not noticed that? She wiped her tears away and pulled a pillow over her head. "Leave me alone. Go away. You have sweatpants now. Sneak in through the back. No one cares."

"Still not leaving." Instead, he crawled into bed with her, pulling her back to his front. "Staying here with you."

"You're making me mad." Her body tightened, but it wasn't anger. She recognized the anticipation pulsing through her veins. Desire.

"It's what I do." His voice was gentle.

"Would it help if I said I don't want you here?"

He tugged her closer. "You kept my sweatpants."

She had a feeling he'd read something into that. "What was I supposed to do? Burn them?"

He laughed. "Stranger things have happened."

She harrumphed, trying not to enjoy the feel of his warm, tough arms around her, pulling her tight to him.

"I'm sorry I got mad, baby." Then his lips went to her neck, and he buried his face there. "It's just that…I've lost so much in my life. Can't lose you, too."

She bit her quivering lower lip to push the tears back. Luke *had* lost so much in his first eighteen years of life.

She'd lost their baby. That part would forever be her fault. For not going to the doctor early enough to get pre-natal pills, and everything else she should have done. Gran and her sisters claimed that wasn't true, not at all, that it couldn't possibly have been Lexi's fault, but she wouldn't believe it.

She'd had something wonderful and precious once and hadn't managed to take care of it. She'd lost the baby. End of story.

And now, she wanted to cry because Luke was being too nice. He was taking care of her when she didn't deserve it. She'd ask him to leave again, but it would be useless. Once Luke made up his mind, it would take a tornado to move him two inches.

"The thing is, if we'd had our baby, we would have been the center of gossip. Do you ever stop to think about that?"

"Wouldn't have been if we got married like I wanted."

"Exactly, but I didn't want you to marry me because you thought you *had* to." She stiffened in his arms.

All of this was difficult to think about, much less say out loud because Sabrina's humiliation should have been small compared to what might have been Lexi's. At the very least to their parents. Sabrina had rarely been able to see the only boyfriend she'd ever had, and not at all after he'd shipped off to Iraq. But her bubbly personality was such that it wasn't difficult to believe she was the loose and wild sister.

Not Lexi.

"Tell me you don't feel guilty about Sabrina." His arms tightened around her.

She turned in his arms to face him. "I try not to, but I should have been a better sister. Maybe taken her phone away after she met that guy. Should have noticed that she was lonely and with the way she loves men, she'd eventually get into trouble. But I was too busy being in love."

He didn't speak, but went up on one elbow and simply gazed at her with those deep brown eyes that told her it had been the same for him. Too busy being in love to realize that the rest of their small and tight world was about to shatter and about to break.

A ragged breath came out of her. "Why didn't you cry about our baby?"

"I did. Just not in front of you." Pain flashed in his eyes.

That sounded just like him, so she shouldn't have been too surprised by the statement. Yet she was. "Do you blame me?"

"Never. I can't believe you're even asking me that."

"We never talked about it. We moved on since the baby hadn't been part of the plan anyway. But I don't know who else to blame. You blamed yourself for your mother, and that wasn't your fault, either."

"Yeah. Guess there are some things we just can't control no matter how hard we try."

"That's what Gram always says."

"A wise lady."

"I'm sorry about the baby," she said, as a solid ache pulsed through her heart. "I never told you that."

"I'm sorry, too." He moved her even closer. "Go to sleep, honey. I've got you."

So, she lay there and sobbed. She hadn't cried this much for at least a year, if not longer. She cried about Maggie Wyatt, cried about the baby, and about losing her father too soon. Cried about being dumped by the label because of one mistake after so many years of being their perfect little country gold angels. She cried about losing Luke to the road. Then she cried because she was so damned selfish for wanting him all to herself.

And by the time she was all cried out, she finally fell asleep.

CHAPTER 13

"It's you. It's always been you." ~ Meme

W hen Lexi pushed one swollen eyelid open what seemed like minutes later, night had fallen. A shaft of moonlight poured through the slats of her window blinds. She rubbed her eyes, wondering how long she'd been out. Luke was no longer in bed with her, but she heard noises coming from her kitchen. Throwing the covers back, she climbed out of bed and tiptoed into the kitchenette. There she found Luke, his naked back to her, standing over her stove, making the tiny kitchen area seem so much smaller.

He turned. "You hungry?"

It was then that she noticed he'd made grilled cheese sandwiches, which, as it turned out, was about the only thing Luke could cook. Fortunately, his grilled cheese was delicious. He'd used a ton of butter and just the right amount of cheese.

"Um—"

"Yeah, you're hungry." He put one on a plate and cut it in half.

She listened to the loud crunch of bread as he sliced, that's how crispy he made them. If she hadn't been hungry before that, she was now. All the sobbing had tired her out, but now that she'd slept enough, the hunger pangs were real. She'd had nothing but coffee and hot dogs all day. She wasn't hungry. Try famished.

Still, she stood by the two-person kitchen table, and her finger traced the edge. "I guess I'm a *little* hungry," she lied.

He pulled out a stool with his foot, and she sat. Then, he placed one amazingly perfect grilled cheese on a plate in front of her. She took one bite and closed her eyes in pleasure. The combination of crispy, buttery bread and melted American cheese were just utter perfection. When she opened her eyes, Luke was staring at her, an amused look on his face.

"Aren't you going to eat one?"

"Ate while you were sleeping."

"You shouldn't have let me sleep so long." She stretched, feeling the movement in every one of her tired muscles.

"You needed it."

She ate in silence for a few minutes, Luke sitting across from her on the other stool. His phone pinged. And pinged. Each time, he picked it up, glanced at it, then put it back down.

"Aren't you going to respond?"

"It can wait."

"You can go ahead and ping them back. Whoever it is."

"It's just Gary.

"Then it could be important."

He locked gazes with hers. "It can wait."

That explained a lot. "Is that what you told yourself when I pinged you? She can wait."

A flash of irritation passed in his dark gaze. "No. This is what I'm telling myself now that I'm trying to restore balance."

"Is that what you're doing here in Whistle Cove? Restoring balance or writing songs?"

His gaze cut into hers. "What I'm doing here is taking care of you like I always have, like I'm never going to stop doing."

"I don't want to argue with you." She stood up and placed her plate in the sink.

Turning to thank him, she also got ready to tell him to leave when he pulled her into his lap. "Baby."

The words were said so tenderly that a tingle went up her spine. "Luke, stop—"

His dark eyes were taking her in, every bit of her. Quietly assessing, gauging his chances. And this was the time for raw honesty.

She gave it to him. "I'm still a little mad at you."

"I know you are." His arms tightened around her. "And I get that."

She couldn't help threading her fingers through his thick dark hair. He'd always had her heart, from the time he'd first claimed her as his own. "But...I'm working on it."

"Yeah?" His hand lowered to the small of her back and gently caressed her.

"I didn't like seeing you with those other women."

"Understood. Didn't like it when you did a duet with Brett Ellis that one time."

He would bring that up. Sabrina had the flu, so Lexi had been tasked with singing a duet with the handsome singer at a CMA show one year.

"Why? He was a perfect gentleman."

"If by that you mean he couldn't stop staring at your ass, then I agree."

She snorted. "Stop it. He did not."

"You would think that. That's because you've never noticed when guys checked you out, but I sure in the hell did."

"It was just business."

"So was my stuff." He held her gaze. In those deep brown eyes she didn't see a hint of deception.

He was here now when he didn't have to be. Taking care of her.

She pressed her forehead to his. "I know, honey. I've known for a while."

He let out a breath. "Fucking finally."

A small laugh escaped her, and she put a finger over his lips. "Don't curse. We got you over that bad habit once. Let's not do it again."

After dinner, Luke checked on the clothes he'd hung to dry out. They were still damp, so he sent her to bed and turned on the TV, the volume low. A few minutes later, he was tuning her guitar.

She rolled over on her elbow and faced the front room. "Don't you have to get up early for the morning show? Aren't they sending a car?"

"I might just stay up all night. Easier."

"You're going to be exhausted."

"Getting used to it." He strummed a chord, the guitar now in perfect tune.

She heard him flipping through channels as she tossed and turned and tried to get comfortable with Luke half-naked in the next room.

"Luke?" She finally asked, because there was no other way she would sleep at all. "Could you lay down with me until I fall asleep?"

"Sure, baby."

And just like that, once he'd pulled her back to his stomach, it was probably seconds before she drifted off.

LEXI WOKE up the next morning because her back was cold.

And Luke was gone.

He hadn't even woken her, and she'd been so exhausted and worn out that she didn't remember so much as budging all night. Now, she tore off the covers, hopped out of bed, and ran to the TV to see if she could catch his interview. Once she flipped to the local station for *Good Morning, Monterey Bay*, she saw Luke on the screen, strumming his acoustic guitar. The interview portion, and she had to assume there'd been one, must have completed, and now they'd talked him into singing a song. That song was, of *course*, *Falling for Forever*.

After not hearing it for months, she now listened to it for the second time in about as many days. The acoustic version was breathtaking, seeing as that's how he'd come up with the melody in the first place. It took her back to the first time she'd heard him strum the chord progression, and deep in her bones known he had something special. But even she had no idea the song would be so well received.

She stared at the man who just hours earlier had been next to her in bed. He'd stayed up all night. No one would be able to tell. There was no trace of fatigue or exhaustion in his eyes. The camera loved Luke Wyatt. Someone at the label had seen that and run with it. She didn't blame them.

The label had worked hard to polish Luke Wyatt into exactly what they needed him to be: a virile and handsome country singer, even if he'd grown up by the ocean, worked the fishing boats, and hung out with some rough characters. Even with a father like Reggie Wyatt. All that added to the element of *bad boy gone good,* always helpful when packaging a male artist.

When Luke had to become the front person overnight, when his chance had finally arrived, it came along with fame lessons and a speech coach hired by the label. Luke had stopped dropping the F bomb and learned how to smooth talk with the best of them. He'd learned how to control his temper better.

Excited about the morning, Lexi showered and dressed in her work jeans, a sky-blue sweater, and her favorite kickass ankle boots. She wondered if Sabrina or Jessie had seen the interview, and what they thought. Wondered what they'd say about the fact that Luke had pushed his way back into her life again, and she'd let him. She had no idea what it meant, or if they'd ever be what they'd once been to each other. But for now, she was willing to explore it.

Lexi swung by Olga's kitchen to grab a mug of coffee.

"Did you see Mr. Luke this morning on the TV?" Olga asked.

"I missed the beginning, but I saw him singing." She added exactly three tablespoons of her liquid creamer. No more, no less.

"He's so talented!"

How could she argue with the obvious? Lexi patted Olga's back in silent agreement. Next, Lexi headed to Jessie's office for their weekly morning meeting on the status of all things Wilder, which these days, was just the B&B.

"You don't have a room for your *mother?*"

Lexi stopped in her tracks when she heard the pitchy, whiny voice of Elizabeth "Kit" Wilder.

Mom.

"I'm sorry, we're just completely booked. Maybe you can stay with me in my cottage. Or Lexi's. Or Sabrina's," Jessie's soft voice said. "You could have called first."

Lexi took two more cautious steps toward the office door and considered whether she should just turn around and make a run for it. Her morning was great so far, and she hated to ruin her forward trajectory.

"*Call*? Are you or are you *not* my daughter? Because I clearly recall fourteen hours of labor. Back labor! I'm a Wilder, honey, and as such I deserve the courtesy of a room at the *Wilder* B&B!"

"But—"

"Hi, Mom," Lexi said as she entered the room. She had to save her sister, after all.

"Lexi! Sweetie!" Kit turned to look up at Lexi, a huge smile on her face.

Uh-huh. She wanted something. Lexi just wasn't sure what yet.

Kit Wilder was a dead ringer for Samantha Jones from *Sex and the City*. She dressed at the height of fashion when she could, and today wore a white A-line dress with a slender black belt, and gorgeous gold sandals with a loop that ran around her ankle several times. She was fifty but looked forty. Therefore she didn't think it was a big deal to lie about her age. Even if the age at which she would have had to give birth to her girls became younger every year. Pretty soon, she'd have to claim to have been a child bride.

"Jessie tells me there's no room at the inn! It's not even Christmas. How can that be true?" Kit laughed at her tasteless joke, and Jessie, ever the people pleaser, did too.

"Mom, it *is* true." Lexi straightened. "Jessie has worked hard to get us out of the red. And now we have a long wait list and no vacancy."

"And what does your grandmother have to say about that?" Mom sniffed. "Surely, she doesn't want her only daughter-in-law thrown out on the streets."

"Mom, seriously. On the *streets*? You can stay with me. Anyway, what are you *doing* here?" Lexi asked.

"I'm visiting my daughters. Is that so strange?"

But Mom had stayed away for the better part of the year they'd been off the road and finding their way, choosing to stay in Palm Springs where she'd lived with Dad until he'd passed away. She had a condo there and friends who doled out plenty of sympathy. She'd constantly moaned about her lot in life as a young widow but, 'that's what happens when you marry a man fourteen years your senior.'

It had actually only been a ten-year age difference, but as Mom's age remained static, and she never got any older, that age difference stretched.

Sabrina walked into the office then, wearing her Mrs. Hippy costume. A tie-dyed ankle length sundress, layers of necklaces that she chimed when she moved, and a peace+love purple bandanna over her forehead. Blue round shaped sunglasses glasses that perched on the edge of her nose completed the look.

"Momma!" She squealed and opened her arms wide.

"Baby girl!" Kit stood, opened her arms, and Sabrina threw herself into the embrace.

Mom then pulled her back and took a long and appraising look at the get-up. "What on *earth* are you wearing?"

"It's my flower child costume. Do you like it?" She spun around.

Sabrina had always been Mom's favorite. Lexi and Jessie didn't much mind that, seeing as they'd pretty much been Dad's favorites. But since Sabrina and Mom had so much in common, and her sister clearly needed her momma, it only made sense. Fashion sense, and its importance, was merely the beginning of a long list of commonalities with her youngest.

"Nice, sweetie, but I think you can do better." Mom gave another assessing look at the get-up.

"I'm in hiding. It's my disguise," Sabrina said.

Mom went hand on hip and leaned back. "You're not doing *that* again."

One good thing Lexi could say about her mother was that she was a Mama Bear in every sense of the word. While she might have issues with her daughters, and she did, often, no one else on earth was allowed to criticize. At least not in her presence. She still wasn't speaking to half of the residents of Whistle Cove. People she and Dad had grown up with. Kit had once threatened to sue Mrs. Oppenheimer for slander and made the old lady cry. It could get ugly at times because Mom 'didn't suffer fools.' Her words.

"I don't know." Sabrina shrugged. "It's kinda fun."

"We'll go shopping. And to the spa for manicures and pedis! It's been a while since we had a girl's day." Mom clasped her hands together.

"Oh, wow! That would be such fun. When?"

"We could go today, but I need to get situated. Jessie says I don't have a room." Mom stuck her bottom lip out in a pout.

"You don't have a room for Momma?" Sabrina turned to Jessie.

"We're booked," Jessie said. "Remember?"

"You can stay with me!" Sabrina put both hands on Mom's shoulders. "It will be like a long slumber party."

"Oh, honey. I guess we can do that for a bit, but since I'll be staying a while, we should probably get me my own room. Those cottages are so small, we'll be right on top of each other."

They were actually perfect for two, but Lexi kept her mouth shut.

"How long are you staying?" Lexi and Jessie both asked at once.

"Does a month sound okay?" She smiled at Sabrina, knowing clearly who would be happy and who would not.

"A month. That's awesome!" Sabrina jumped up and down. "You should really move here. Maybe you can move into Gran's big house if she marries Sir Clint."

Mom's right eye twitched. "Sir Clint?"

She probably wouldn't like the fact that Gran had a boyfriend while Kit was still "'Saving myself for the right man, after my precious John. A hard act to follow, you know.'"

"That's Gran's new boyfriend. We have so much to talk about. C'mon, I'll take you to my cottage and give you a couple of dresser drawers and some closet space." Lexi pulled Mom's hand.

Lexi resisted face palming. This was so not going to work out for Mom, who had a wardrobe built over the years that wouldn't even fit in one of their small closets, much less half of one. It was clear she'd want a room of her own, a suite preferably, where she could pretend she was a paying guest.

"Alright, let's do that, dear. Meanwhile, your sisters will find me a room. Maybe you could move someone around. Or cancel someone." Mom waved a hand dismissively.

"That's bad for business," Lexi bit out.

"Well, what about Luke's room?" Mom said without missing a beat.

Lexi froze. Kit knew Luke was here. It had been only a week. "How…how did you know?"

"I'm on Friendbook. I tweet."

"Then you should know that Luke is the one who's brought us a zero-vacancy rate and a wait list." Lexi glared at her mother.

"But why does he need a room all to himself? Can't he stay with you?" she asked.

For once, Lexi had no words. Finally, only one came out, somewhere between a hiss and a roar: "*Mom!*"

She wagged her finger. "Don't you 'mom' me. You two spent years on the road sharing a bed, keeping both me and my poor John in the dark I might add, and now you can't spend a few weeks sharing a cottage?"

While Lexi silently tried to absorb 'a few weeks' she swallowed the guilt she had often felt about living with Luke on the tour bus with her clean and wholesome image. But she'd been madly in love with the man, and allowances should be made for that.

"We broke up." Mom had the full 411, so why she pretended not to know this information only infuriated Lexi.

"You're still friends, aren't you?" The look in her sea green eyes was positively hopeful.

Oh, the irony.

Kit had never been Luke's champion, secretly hoping Lexi would wind up marrying country music royalty. Mom had several men in mind, all of them about twenty years Lexi's senior. The only reason Mom would be interested in Lexi's relationship with Luke now meant she saw him as country gold hot and she wanted some of that to now rub off on her daughters. That made Lexi feel strangely protective of him. She didn't want the music industry to play any part in whatever had started again between her and Luke.

"They might not be friends much longer if they have to share that closet," Jessie piped in, obviously uncomfortable with the heavy silence in the room following Mom's words. "Just sayin'."

Sabrina laughed in agreement. "Hell, yeah."

Lexi and her mother were still locked in a staring contest.

"We're *friends*. We're not sleeping together," Lexi eventually stated.

That wasn't exactly true, of course. They'd actually slept

together last night. *Sleeping* being the operating word. Not that she would share that with Kit.

Pulling Mom away, Sabrina tried to lighten the mood and the clash of wills. "C'mon, Momma. Let's go get a facial. You'll feel better after that."

CHAPTER 14

"The truth is, bad decisions lead to interesting stories." ~ Meme

The limo the station sent dropped off Luke at the entrance to the B&B, and he made his way up the stone walkway. Glancing to the deck, he pulled off his shades in disbelief. True, he was currently the definition of tired, but he had to be seeing things. But no, on closer inspection, there sat Kit Wilder at a table on the wide wrap around deck that faced the ocean. As usual, she dressed like a movie star. He'd never much cared for the woman and the airs she put on. But the worst thing about Kit Wilder was the way she treated people who couldn't help or advance her daughters' careers.

Luke knew the country music grapevine rumors well: from the moment the Wilder Sisters had crashed and burned, Kit had been trying to find a way to get one or all of them back in the spotlight for a second chance. A "come back" she called it, just like "those athletes do" and to her mind, one had been in the works since the moment the label had dropped them. But Kit didn't have the connections that her late husband had in the business. She'd been less than successful in her venture, not that Luke thought that would stop her. One thing he could say about Kit Wilder was that she adored her daughters and wanted the best for them. Unfortunately, she'd be the one to decide what was best for them, thank you very much.

And for Lexi, that had never been Luke Wyatt.

Did he sound bitter? Maybe a little. Luke bristled every time he was forced to be around her. The more she had hated on him, the more jealous he'd become over Lexi's time. It was the insecurity that had ruled him then. The nagging thought that he wasn't good enough to be with Lexi. A secret Kit had to know. Now, he couldn't say that he and Kit didn't have something in common for once. They both wanted Lexi back in the business where she belonged. Back in Nashville. They both thought they could make decisions for Lexi. The difference was that Luke didn't honestly believe he could always be successful at that, while he had little doubt Kit remained downright convinced she could.

"Luke!" She waved in his direction, meaning he wasn't going to escape her claws. Not today.

He wanted a few hours of sleep more than he wanted his next breath, since his back ached like a bitch. He'd pulled an all-nighter again. First, he'd watched Lexi sleep, played with her hair until he thought his clothes might be dry enough, then sneaked back into his pink room in still somewhat damp clothes to shower and change. But he couldn't ignore Kit.

Didn't mean he had to be friendly.

He came up to her table, and whipped off his shades. "Mrs. Wilder."

She didn't take off her huge circular sunglasses, preferring to stay reclusive and mysterious, he supposed.

"Son, call me Kit. How many times have I asked you to do that?"

Try exactly none. Luke didn't say that, but instead slipped his glasses back on. "Sorry. Forgot. How've you been?"

"Oh, you know. Horrible. Nothing is the same without John."

Luke would have to agree. John Wilder had been one of a kind and Luke had thought of him as a father. He still missed their nightly after-show talks. Like Luke, Mr. Wilder had been a night owl. They'd had conversations which had taught Luke as much about the music industry as how to be a good husband, father, and family man.

He'd been the father Luke wished he'd had.

"Miss him, too."

He was then treated to a long speech about life without John. Life without the music industry. Life constantly defending her 'baby girl' who made an innocent mistake, and those horrible people who had fooled themselves into thinking they were better because they'd never sexted. Luke was a little bit freaked out that she knew the term.

"I'm waiting for my baby girl now. We're going down to Lulu's for a spa day. We never splurge these days. But I figure she's long overdue, and I know I am."

He knew that 'baby girl' meant Sabrina, so he didn't have to ask. Also, he didn't believe that Kit was overdue for a spa day, but what the hell did he know?

Luke stood up, sensing an early exit strategy. "Well, I'll leave you to it."

"Oh, sit down. She's going to take forever to change."

Reluctantly, Luke sat back down, picturing his bed longingly and wondered if Kit would notice if he listened with his eyes closed.

"My baby was in some ridiculous get-up dressed like a flower child, so no one would recognize her. I insisted she change into her cutest dress to go out with her mother. She

144

won't hide who she is around me." At this, she lowered her shades to meet his eyes. "Do you think that's fair, Luke?"

He never had. "Absolutely not."

She sighed. "It's a man's world. A girl likes sex, she's a slut. A man likes sex, he's a stud. Am I right?"

Talking about sex with his girlfriend's mother hadn't ever been among the top ten conversations Luke wanted to have in his life. "Um, sure."

"How are you and Lexi doing?"

Luke had hoped to get to this subject. Right about now, he was Kit's answer to prayer, and now she could be his. He could bring Lexi back into the business. Seeing as he hoped to take her to Nashville, kicking and screaming if he had to, this might be a better option. Getting the support of her mother.

"We're talking again." He leaned back in his seat, closing his eyes.

"Wonderful!"

He didn't have to have his eyes open to hear the joy emanating off her.

"I always knew you two would be good together."

Luke decided to pretend he didn't know otherwise. Pretend he didn't know Kit had been staunchly on the anyone but Luke train for years. She'd changed her mind, and while he was somewhat disgusted by why, he wasn't too proud to use it to his advantage. It was different than using his fame to get a better table at a restaurant or to cut in line. This was about getting the only woman he'd ever loved back for good. He'd do anything.

He cleared his throat. "Yeah, thanks. Me too."

"I'm happy for your immense success. John always believed in you. Knew you had it in you to strike out on your own."

Luke knew that to be true because John had said that very

thing to Luke many times. For years, he hadn't wanted to leave his position with the Wilder Sisters band to go off on his own. The timing hadn't been right. He hadn't had enough original material. There were too many other factors to consider. And Lexi, who had wanted him around. Lexi, for whom he'd literally do anything.

"I hate the way it happened."

"We all do." She reached over to pat his hand. "It all got out of control so fast. Had John been around, none of this would have happened. He'd have found a way to recover from the set back."

Kit didn't seem to realize that at least Lexi didn't necessarily consider it a setback, since she'd gotten a break from the constant pressure of the road. "I feel like Lexi might be enjoying the time off."

"Of course, because she hasn't yet realized that she can be a *star* all on her own. All of my girls could be. Separate and unique talents, and better together, but fine apart, too. John was a family man to the core, so he wanted us all to be in this business together, travel together, and be a family. It was great when the girls were younger, but as they got to be successful young adults, we had less control."

Oh, he did know that.

Sabrina joined them a few minutes later, giving Luke a breezy greeting in the form of a half wave, half salute. "Ready to go."

Kit beamed. "You look beautiful. That's what I like to see."

"We're having a spa day!" Sabrina said to Luke with the kind of enthusiasm reserved for Christmas.

"I heard," Luke said with a smile.

He said goodbye to Kit and Sabrina and headed to his room, but not without being asked for an autograph five times on his way. Then, paranoid he was being followed, and worried he'd have guests camped outside his door, he took a long and circuitous route to his room. Once certain no one noticed him, he let himself inside the room, and collapsed face first on to the bed, fully clothed and not giving a rat's ass.

And finally, he slept.

A FEW HOURS LATER, Luke woke up, showered, and dressed. He was a man on a mission and didn't need to waste any time. It was early afternoon, and he found Lexi out on the deck, chatting with some of the visitors. She pointed to a map, probably giving directions to the Monterey Bay Aquarium, Cannery Row, or any number of local touristy attractions.

He positioned himself a few feet away, so as not to interrupt, but so that she'd clearly see him waiting.

She laughed and tossed back her long hair, then caught his eyes and shyly looked away. After a few more words to the visitors, she waved to them and headed in his direction.

"Hi," she said, stepping into his line of sight.

"Hi, baby." He propped his shades on his head. "You sleep well?"

"Thanks to you."

"Good." He took her hand and threaded his fingers through hers. "Any chance you might need help getting to sleep again?"

She smiled. "Maybe."

"I'm on call for that service. Just say the word."

"Ping you?" she teased.

"I won't ignore *your* pings."

"What did Gary want, anyway?"

"To remind me to behave on TV. Like I needed the reminder. Asked me to watch my mouth. Guess he thought being back home, I might revert back to my old 'bad boy' ways."

"We can't have that."

"Well, *you* can have that." He met her gaze, suspecting she probably knew exactly what he meant.

By the flush on her cheeks, she did. She'd been shy with him from the moment they'd met, which he'd found attractive. Once, he'd believed that Lexi only wanted him because she was slumming. Either way, he didn't care. He already knew she was too good for him. But he hadn't been too lucky in his life, so when Lexi loved him, and loved him so good he thought he'd landed in heaven on a day pass, he shut his mouth. Kept it closed. If she thought him to be good enough for her, he wasn't going to try to convince her otherwise.

He tugged her into his arms and ran his hand down to the small of her back. She looked up at him, eyes sparkling and shining, and his pulse sped up, hammering away in his chest. He lowered his head to close the distance between them.

"We have an audience," she whispered near his lips.

She tipped her head back and turned. He followed her line of sight, and sure enough a small crowd of onlookers had formed. When he caught them staring, some were kind enough to look away. Others were bolder and continued to stare, mouths gaping. He turned her, so that her back was facing all of them and was about to suggest he and Lexi meet inside for some privacy, when Jessie came running outside, headed straight for Lexi.

She waved a cellphone. "You have to go get Mom and Sabrina. They're downtown and causing some kind of scene at Lulu's Day Spa. My friend Donnie from the pet supply store just called me. It's bad."

"I'll head right over." Lexi pulled the rest of the way out of his arms, or as far as she could get when he didn't let go.

"I'm coming with you." He tugged on her hand and led the way. "I'll drive."

"No. You don't need to get in the middle of whatever drama my Mom's cooked up this time," Lexi said.

"I said I'll drive."

"I'm not driving in that deluxe sedan."

"Give me your keys." He held out his palm.

"No! I'm driving."

"Lexi—"

"Oh my god, you two. Just like old times. Stop arguing and just move!" Jessie gave Lexi a little shove.

He followed Lexi to her cottage where she ran inside to grab the keys to her truck and reluctantly tossed them to him. Driving them downtown, he saw the scene when they were more than a block away. So did Lexi, going by the hitch in her breath.

"I thought we were done with all this. Leave it to Mom," Lexi said.

"How long has this been going on?" He searched for a parking space to no avail.

Whistle Cove was a small town that had grown up too fast, considering it was situated in the heart of the diamond that was Monterey Bay. A crowd had gathered in front of the storefront, surrounding both mother and daughter. Most observed passively, holding up phones with assumed looks on their faces.

One look at Sabrina's cowering form as she stood slightly behind her mother, and Luke wanted to get in the middle of it all and address the situation. The old Luke, Reggie's son, would have done that, hands-down. Put himself between Lexi, her sisters, and anyone who even considered hurting them. And while he realized that hauling off and slugging someone might be bad publicity, ask him how much he cared right now.

"It's been mostly quiet for a while, but leave it to Mom to bring this mess all back up again," Lexi said. "She loves the drama."

Luke was still trying to angle for a parking space two storefronts down when Lexi unbuckled and flew out the passenger door before he could hold her back.

"Lexi, damn it all."

That left him with little choice but to double park.

"Ladies, you both calm down now," a man Luke didn't recognize said from the sidelines.

"Iris, you started it," said a woman with rollers in her hair. "Why don't you just get over your damned self?"

"Kit didn't *do* anything," someone else said. "Leave her girl alone."

A contingent had apparently left the spa to watch the side show attraction, which appeared to be just between two women. One of them, of course, was Kit.

"You take that back, Iris! No one talks to my daughter that way. No. One." Kit waved animatedly. "Are you so perfect, huh? Huh? Are you?"

"Better than you are, anyway. You can fool some people in hoity-toity Palm Springs, but we went to high school together. I know you're *fifty* and still dressing like you're thirty. No wonder your daughter is loose. Look at her example!"

Oh, man. Huge mistake. Luke knew before he'd crossed the street that he would be in the middle of some major damage control after this. The minute the crowd noticed him, phones angled away from Sabrina and Kit to him.

"No one says that to my Momma!" Sabrina went for the woman, stopped only by Lexi, who had managed to get between her and the other woman within seconds.

Lexi managed to get in the middle of the melee in seconds. Arms were waving and swinging, but thankfully, all of the men stayed clear. That made Luke's only job hauling Lexi out of this mess.

"Leave my sister alone!" Lexi shouted, standing between her sister and the woman, and Luke caught her by the waist. "You don't have to be so mean, Iris!"

He held on tight as Lexi jumped and flailed about, hair flying, fists clenched. Bending close to her ear, he whispered. "Be still, baby."

"I see Kit has another daughter who can't control herself," Iris said, shaking her head and smirking.

Lexi made valiant attempt to wrestle him off. "Let me go!"

"Can't." Instead, he lifted her up by her waist and carried her away from the crowd and toward her truck.

"Luke!" she shouted, her hands clawing at his fingers, trying to pry him off. It was not happening.

"Sabrina, Kit. C'mon. Now." He threw a look in Sabrina and Kit's direction. Wisely, they followed him, Kit shielding her daughter with her body.

Outside the front passenger side of the truck, Luke set Lexi down, one arm braced on either side of her, basically locking her in. While Sabrina and Kit climbed into the back seats, Luke tried his best to calm his wild woman down.

He tipped her chin. "Baby, you need to take a breath."

"I— she—" Lexi fought to regain her composure *and* her breath.

Luke could clearly see the strain in her amber eyes. Eyes suspiciously watering as she fought to hold tears back. She was trying. He'd give her that.

"I know. But we're better than her, yeah?" He buried his face in her head of wild hair. "You want to get me arrested?"

When she finally stilled, he used the moment to quickly open the door, push her up inside, click the seatbelt into place, and walk to the other side.

"Hey, aren't you—?" A woman from the crowd said.

By now, everyone watched closely, probably impressed that he'd gotten three Wilder women to agree to anything. "Nah, I just look like him."

He'd now lied for the second time about being himself. Fame could really screw with a man's head.

"Hey, you really do!" The woman said, a big smile on her face.

At that point someone else said, "Are you high? Of course that's Luke Wyatt. He's from Whistle Cove, or did you forget?"

He pulled out back onto the street, but not before Lexi rolled down the window and shouted, "Screw you!"

"Really, babe?" He had managed to roll up the window from his side before she could get all the words out. And locked it.

Lexi had her hand over her mouth, like she couldn't believe what she'd done.

Sabrina dissolved into giggles. "Yeah, screw Iris! She insulted my Momma."

"Oh, honey," Kit said, reaching for Lexi's shoulder. "I'm sorry I lost my temper with awful Iris. She used to be my friend."

"That's okay," Lexi said from the front seat. "You're not the only one to lose her temper."

Luke doubled checked to make sure the backseat windows were locked too. Not many had ever known it to be true, but the Wilder women *could* be wild. All you had to do was mess with one of them. Otherwise, they all did fair imitations of saints. Other than Sabrina, of course.

"No," Mrs. Wilder said to Sabrina. "No one but your husband is going to see that hinney of yours."

"Right, Momma." Sabrina settled down.

And in his rearview mirror, Luke caught Kit's proud smile.

CHAPTER 15

"Dear heart: stop getting involved in everything. Your job is to pump blood. That's it." ~ Meme

*L*exi had managed to breathe evenly by the time Luke drove them back to the B&B. Mostly. When Iris had insulted both her mother *and* her sister, Lexi's stomach got so tight that she couldn't remember much else after that.

"Let's go walk on the beach," Mom said now as Luke pulled in by the cottages.

"After I go change," Sabrina said.

Lexi's heart seized. Her sister was dressed in a short, pink, flowery sundress that went to just above her knees. Nothing in the slightest bit provocative. She wore matching strappy pink sandals that didn't even have a heel.

"Don't you dare."

Lexi and Mom spoke at once.

"You look sweet," Mom said.

"Really?" Sabrina whispered, and Lexi's heart split again.

Too much. It was all too much.

"Wear what you want, Sabrina," Lexi spit out. "Otherwise, you let them win."

Smart man that he was, Luke stayed silent on the driver's side. He had a lot to answer for right now, such as his pushy caveman ways. But she'd deal with *him* later.

"Oh. Okay." Sabrina swung open the door and slowly got out of the truck. "Thanks, Luke, for the rescue."

"Not a problem." He twisted in his seat to give Sabrina a smile.

"Yes, thank you for saving us from ourselves. Both of you." Kit reached to squeeze Luke's shoulder with one hand and Lexi's with the other. "Always been such a great team."

Lexi bit back a reply to that and waited as Mom and Sabrina exited the vehicle and shut the doors. Then she whipped her head toward Luke. "You!"

He slowly turned his lowered head to study her from underneath his lashes. "Yeah?"

She drilled a finger into his chest. "What makes you think you can pick me up and physically move me like that?"

Luke didn't look the slightest bit apologetic. "History."

"*History?* What does that mean?"

"Mine. My history. This is the kind of situation I've been in dozens of times before. Especially right after Reggie got arrested, and before he went to trial. Some of his so-called friends tried to intimidate me from going up on the witness stand to testify against him. This might be right in front of Lulu's Day Spa and not the waterfront, but some things don't change. Situations escalate, and they run out of control fast."

She didn't know what to say to that. It was true that this was Luke's area of expertise, and also true that Lexi had never been involved in a cat fight. Not unless you wanted to count one hair-pulling incident in third grade. Thinking this might be a good time to exit, and end this conversation, she stretched out her hand for the keys Luke had pulled out of the ignition. He met her eyes, set them in her palm and closed her fingers. She stared at him another minute, the beautiful boy she'd loved since she was eighteen years old. Her heart gave an unwilling tug.

She turned to leave, but his hand was on her free wrist, the one closest to him.

"What?" She turned, annoyed because this had started off as a great day and spiraled into something…less than desirable. It had all started with her mother's arrival, which she might have guessed was the harbinger of trouble ahead.

"Don't think for a second that I didn't believe you could have handled yourself."

"Yeah?" She leaned back a little bit in the seat because this was certainly interesting information. For a year now, she'd wanted to be brave. It struck her that she was now finally in a place where she didn't allow her own guilt to stop her from fighting back.

"You were handling yourself so well, that I worried you were going to handle yourself right into a jail cell for the night. And then where would I be?"

The tenderness in his eyes as he said those words went straight through her heart and sliced it with a sweet, clean cut. "Luke—"

"Tell you exactly where I'd be. Getting you bailed out. Then you would be pissed at me for using my money to bail you out because you seem to think my money can't be used to help you in any way."

"That's not—"

"Don't try to argue that." He held up a hand. "You see now why I had to step in, pull you out of that mess before you clocked someone."

That shocked her to the core. She, Alexis Wilder, could never ever actually *hurt* someone. And Luke knew that better than anyone. "You know I couldn't have done that."

"I know when it comes to your sisters, you're like a lion, ready to take on the world. Don't even try to tell me different." He sat back, spreading his long arm out, reaching behind her seat.

"You know me well. I guess I should thank you. You saved the day…again." She felt more than a little contrite. "First towing me out of the water, next out of a fight. Lately you're always pulling me out of stuff."

"Baby, don't do that." His fingers moved up to curl around her neck. "Don't act like this is your fault."

She stiffened her spine. "I'm not. It's just that…we've been dealing with this fallout for so long. I want it to be over already. Sabrina was just a silly girl, on the road for half her life, and one boyfriend her whole life. I hate that all it takes is one lousy person to make her feel so small."

"I hate it, too."

Just one look in his soft gaze, and she understood it to still be true. "I know you do."

She studied his dark-eyed gaze, and knew if she didn't get out of this truck, she would attack him. She climbed out of the truck, and so did he.

"What are you doing now?" Lexi said.

"Going to lock myself in my room and write some more songs. Check in with Gary and let him know I didn't screw up the interview this morning. It being a local station, he didn't think he would be able to watch the show."

"I did."

Oh well, she hadn't meant to admit that and blurt it out like she'd been given a truth serum. What next? Admit she fantasized about Luke in her bed again, doing more than holding her while she slept?

"Yeah?" That seemed to please him, and he gave a slow smile. "Did I do alright?"

She blinked at a ray of sunlight hitting his hair just so, making the brown shine with a hint of copper. "You always do. The label should be proud. You're polished. You're a true pro."

He cocked his head and studied her. "Why do I get the feeling you think that's a bad thing?"

"I...it's not."

"Try again. You were never good with lies."

"You're talking to someone who knows all about branding and packaging. That's why we were sold as the sweet country sister act." She took a breath. "And you can see what happened there."

"You think I'm not going to be able to live with my bad boy gone good image long term?"

"No." She pressed her palm to his chest, to let him know the next words meant something to her. "I just think you're much more than that."

How was Luke supposed to have a normal life when they'd presented him as the bad boy that he wasn't? Luke had never been in jail or an outlaw, but his father was. And the label had simply used that tragedy to their advantage. With a splash of the bad boy who couldn't help his sordid past to attract a mostly female audience. Risky. Dark and handsome. Mysterious.

They'd left the heart out of the equation. In order for Luke to mature as an artist and have a real long-term future, he'd have to go beyond that. Dig deep. But Lexi understood the powers that be had tunnel vision. They were mostly interested in the present. Only interested in money and sales. And they'd packaged the handsome and virile Luke as a cross between Sam Hunt and Johnny Cash. He had the voice of Thomas Rhett, the good looks of Sam Hunt, along with the outlaw image.

"Thanks, baby." Luke reached and tucked a random hair

behind her ear. "Means a whole lot to me for you to think that."

She needed to get inside her cottage before she jumped Luke. "Okay. I have to get back to work. There are towels and sheets to wash and fold."

"Right."

Her key went to the door and unlocked it. "And Luke? Sorry about my mom. It's pretty obvious what she's trying to do. She never liked you, but now you're her ticket to get us back in the music business, especially Sabrina. Though I don't think she's quite ready yet. But maybe someday."

"Lexi, you know I'll do anything to help that happen. Use whatever connections I have. *Anything*. I owe the Wilder Sisters big time."

She turned to him and stilled. "You don't *owe* me anything."

"Hell, I didn't mean—" One arm went above her shoulder to brace against the door.

She wouldn't look at him. "I know you didn't."

Lowering his face to hers, he wrapped his free hand around the nape of her neck. "Need help sleeping tonight?"

Sleeping. The last thing she was thinking about at the moment was sleeping with him. As in, curling up next to him and closing her eyes. She wanted to do a whole lot more than sleep. For the past two days, she'd seen traces of the old Luke make their appearance. The frustrating, but strong and amazing man she'd fallen so hard for.

She met his gaze. "No."

"Let me in, Lexi. You won't regret it." His eyes smiled.

"You sure?"

"Bet my Gibson on it."

"That's...that's a big risk to take," she teased. "I've always loved your Gibson."

"Think I don't know it?"

"So, if I regret this," she nodded to her door. "I get your Gibson?"

"Yep." Now both his arms braced on either side of her, pinning her in.

It was afternoon, and she was certain there were still towels and sheets to wash and fold. There always were. It was like the chore that never ended. So, essentially, they'd still be there later. Waiting.

"I'll take that deal." She turned to open the door, and he followed her inside. She threw her keys on the couch, suddenly nervous. "Luke—"

Was that her voice trembling like an out of control vibrato? His name was one syllable and she'd made sound like three. She was hopeless against Luke. Helpless. Like a drowning kitten in a deluge. And she didn't want to be alone anymore. Whether she'd regret this or not, it was happening. She wasn't going to run from him. She wasn't going to run from her feelings.

That scared her to pieces.

"What's wrong?" The smile he'd been wearing slipped off his face. His hands dropped low on her waist, and he tugged her close.

Her arms went around him, hands drifting up to flatten against his abs, which clenched under her touch. Her body hummed in anticipation. "Shh. Don't say anything. Just kiss me."

He tipped her chin and bent low to kiss her. Warm, wet, deep, and lingering. There was nothing tender about the kiss. Nothing tentative. It happened to be exactly the way she wanted it. This. Him. She kissed him back hard, her mouth opening up under his, her fingers threading through his thick dark hair, and then lowering to luxuriate in the feel of his muscles tensing under her fingertips. Her fingers trailed down the length of his back to his waist and back up again. She was getting lost in him.

I've been singing that song all over the country for a year. Now it's your turn.

Go to sleep, honey. I've got you.

Don't think for a second I don't believe you could handle yourself.

I'd have bailed you out.

I'd do anything.

I'm crazy about you.

She refused to think anymore, refused to allow worry or let fear inside this house. The only things she'd let in right now were the two of them. Their assorted baggage, and there was a whole lot of it, was going to stay outside that door. She didn't need forever anymore.

She'd take right now.

They got a little wild as they moved through the living room, making their way to her bed, shedding clothes as they went. She tugged off her sweater. He seemed to barely manage enough patience to unbutton his shirt, losing one of the buttons in the process. She helped pull it off his broad shoulders, branding each one with an open-mouthed kiss. Finally, yes, finally they reached the bedroom, and he eased her onto the bed, covering her with his body.

"Baby, you know I—"

"No promises." She held a finger to his lips. "That's the only way I'll do this. Without any more promises to each other."

She saw another flash of hurt and confusion in his gaze, but this wasn't about him. She didn't know how much she could give him because she didn't know that she had anything left to give. She needed time. More time. She had to figure out the rest of her life, and she'd do it on her own terms.

No one would rush her.

Not even Luke.

"Please, babe," she said, trying on a smile. "Yeah?"

His only agreement to her condition was a hot, branding kiss. It seared her skin as he went about removing the rest of her clothes. Jeans were pulled off then discarded, panties, bra, him kissing every part of her as he went. Neck, arms, breasts, stomach, legs, thighs. And in between her thighs. When his tongue and lips mercilessly licked and teased the most sensitive part of her, she could only writhe under him and fist the sheets. He'd always managed to drive her right out of herself. Right off a damn cliff. She came hard against his lips, bucking and moaning his name. Trying hard to leave some hair on his beautiful head.

"You taste so good." He kissed her stomach as she slowly came back down to earth.

She had no bones left in her body. They'd all melted in his heat.

"Now you." She removed his belt and tugged at the pants he still had on, but he stopped her.

"It's been a long time, and I won't last if you do that to me."

He removed a shiny package from his wallet that Lexi was ecstatic to see. Then he tugged off his pants and boxers and shucked them to the side. When he tore at the condom wrapper with his teeth, she almost came just watching him put it on. It was such a beautiful sight. He stroked himself once and did not break eye contact with her. She licked her lips, her body vibrating with heat. He was so gorgeous, that for a moment, she took him all in. His hard angles, sinewy arms and thighs. His flat abs and light smattering of dark chest hair. He was all man, and she'd missed every part of him. Some parts more than others.

Then he rolled her on top, and in one long and powerful

thrust was deep inside her, making her gasp. The sound of her own voice was a roar in her ears, reminding her of what they were doing. What she'd allowed because she wanted him so desperately. Needed him. He'd pushed her past a place of raw pain. Somehow, she'd made it through. She'd played *that* song, and she hadn't died. It was just a song. It didn't have power over her any longer. She'd thought about their baby for the first time in ages, and he had been there again, like he'd been once before. Taking care of her.

This tonight was all… extra. He guided her in a steady rhythm, holding her hips and driving into her. She clung to his shoulders as his thrusts became harder. Lexi dug her fingernails into her hands to hold tears back. She squeezed her eyes shut against the onslaught, which weighed heavily on her heart. She didn't cry easily, but powerful emotions threatened to pull her under.

No promises. No promises.

"Baby," he said and brought her face to his, hand at the nape of her neck. "Look at me. I need you."

He'd heard her thoughts. She opened her eyes and met his, her lashes damp, and she was certain revealing far too much. This mattered. It wasn't simple or easy. In some ways, they'd grown up together. But they were different people now. A little bit older, a lot more jaded. Despite all that, this, the two of them together just like this… still *worked* for her. Oh, how it worked. She wrenched the thought from her mind. Too scary.

"Luke," she breathed, unable to hold the tide back any longer. "I'm—"

"Wait." He slowed them down right when she was on the brink of coming apart. "Slower."

"No," she said, bucking against him. "Don't want to."

"You will."

He took control then, rolling her underneath him where

his strokes became more even and measured as he intentionally slowed them both down. Even though she knew that what waited for her was bigger and far more intense, in the moment she hated when he took the peak away. Hated when he took his time like he never wanted this to stop. He was patient. She, not so much.

But Luke wanted more. He always had.

By now her body was slick with his sweat and hers mixed together, her face flushed, and hair plastered to her face. She had to look a sight, but Luke's hot gaze made her feel like the hottest woman alive. He whispered hot, dirty words in her ear. Words of what he was doing to her and finally, *finally* he lost his tight control. His eyes glazed over, and he pumped faster. Harder. As if he couldn't help himself. Couldn't hold back any longer. In that reckless space, she met him thrust for thrust, angling her hips, so he'd go deeper inside her.

"Luke—"

Her entire body tightened and convulsed as she came with a fierceness that took her breath. Luke came with her, growling her name, and gripping her so tightly she might bruise later, but she didn't care. She didn't feel any pain, only the incredible sensations rippling through her seizing body, one after another, like a powerful undertow pulling her under and bringing her back up again.

And okay, he was right. It always stung when he took that first crest away from her. When he made her wait to claim it.

But as it turned out time and again, this was always worth waiting for.

CHAPTER 16

"Happy Middle Child Day. Oh, you didn't know it was Middle Child Day? That's all right, neither did anyone else." ~ Meme

*L*uke was wrecked. One hundred percent gone. But in a good way.

Lexi had sprawled on top of him, her head on his chest, one leg thrown over one of his. She slept the way she lived: all in. When they'd first started sleeping together, he couldn't handle the closeness. He needed his space and used to disentangle carefully and not wake her. He used to pry her off him on a regular basis. Who knew that after a few years, he wouldn't know how else to sleep but with her half on top of him?

He rolled to his side and tucked the woman responsible for his current state into his arms. They were both breathing like a locomotive train off the rails. He rubbed her back and tried to calm them both down. Bring them back down to planet Earth. Frankly, if it meant leaving her bed he wasn't at all sure he wanted to *be* sane.

She buried her face in his neck and hope slammed into

his chest, hard and painful. He'd waited months for this. For a year, if he was honest. He'd wanted to get her back even while he'd pretended it didn't matter. While he'd put on a show. It had niggled at him through every city and every sold-out show. Someone was missing. Someone who mattered. Nothing was the same without her. Couldn't be. And now that he had her in his arms, he had to remind himself to slow down. Again.

No promises.

The words stung, but he didn't entirely blame her. Even if he thought the whole break-up would have been a non-issue had she come on the tour with him, he'd been a stupid dude. Overwhelmed by all the female attention and the idea for the first time that maybe he was good enough for her. He'd assumed she would always stick by him. Because she belonged to him, and he'd always belonged to her. But Lexi wasn't like any other woman. She happened to be the perfect woman for him. Loving and caring to everyone, but tough when she had to be.

"You okay?" He pressed a kiss on her forehead.

"Mm. Yeah."

He didn't know how long they both lay there, legs entwined and simply touching each other. Now that he'd been inside her again, he didn't want to push her feelings for him too hard or too fast. She had to come to the realization on her own that they were still good together. They could make this work. Forever.

No promises.

He shifted and spoke against her temple. "Do you want me to go?"

"What?" She froze in his arms. A moment ago, she'd had her fingers trailing through the short hairs on his chest. Everything stopped, and she went up on an elbow. "Why? Do you *want* to go?"

"Hell, no." He ran his palm down the length of her back, not wanting to lose contact. "But that's up to you."

"Oh. Right."

Her voice sounded small, and his chest pinched.

"Were it up to me, I'd stay all night, and we'd do this again. Maybe another three times."

She smirked and rolled on her back. "Three *times*? You think you've got that in you, huh?"

"Just let me get my second wind."

"Okay, but this time I call the shots. And I finish when I *say* I finish." She thumped his chest.

"Whatever you say, baby."

"How's your back?"

Just like her to be concerned about him when, at the moment, he was as relaxed as he'd ever been. "What back?"

"That's not funny." She rolled to her side and splayed her fingers on his abs. "Are you taking care of yourself, or pushing it like you always do?"

He folded his hands behind his neck. "I'll take the fifth."

The last thing he wanted at the moment was to remind Lexi that he was weak in any way. The back injury was something he'd learned to live with, and if over the years it had caused him pain, he could manage it. Occasionally, he took over-the-counter pills when it got bad. While it was true that the long nights and excruciating tour schedule would have been easier to handle without his old injury, he didn't want any special allowances made for him. He would work just as hard and just as long as if he had a perfect spine.

He didn't want to face the fact that he already had a bad back at the ripe old age of twenty-nine.

He'd used the pain to remind himself he was alive. Strong. Something he could always use in any line of work. Once, it had been on the wharf and the boat yards. Next, as a roadie who had lifted more than any doctor would have advised him to do. He was certainly not weak like the kid he'd been when unable to dodge his father's fists, much less return fire. Only once, in all those years of getting between his mother and Reggie, had Luke wound up in the hospital. Only once, but that had been enough.

He'd become used to getting between them and taking the hits for his mother. Reggie's fists hadn't been as tough on him as they had been on his mother. Unfortunately, even that hadn't stopped the inevitable. Perhaps he'd only slowed Reggie down.

"Let me just say that it's very difficult when you try to act like you're indestructible," Lexi said.

"Never said I was."

"That may be true, but it would be nice for you to at least admit when you're in pain."

"And what good is that going to do me?"

"For one thing, it might make the label realize that they can't push you so hard on these ridiculous multi-city tours. They're rough on everybody."

"Not me. I can handle it."

He certainly didn't need Lexi worrying about *him*. Didn't she have enough on her plate worrying about Sabrina, worrying about her grandmother, and the B&B? Worrying about being able to write her own songs again, and sell them, so she could help her grandmother. God knew she wasn't going to let him help. He'd never been anyone she had to worry about. Instead, he was the one who wanted to take care of her.

Once again demonstrating her inability to cut him any slack, she rolled her eyes at him. "Luke, you're now big enough and important enough that you might be able to call your own shots with the label. Did you ever think about that?"

Well crap, actually he hadn't. But when he was willing to

work as hard as the next person, and grateful for the opportunity, it didn't make sense to ask for favors from anyone. "Wait a minute. Is this you now, caring about me? Worried about me? Almost seems like you give a shit."

She threw a pillow at his head and then straddled his hips.

He slowly removed the pillow from his face, gripping her hips in case she got any ideas about moving, and slid her a wicked smile. "This is very convenient. As it happens, just got my second wind."

"I can tell. But seems more convenient for me. At least from where I'm sitting." She wriggled on top of him and pushed on his chest so he'd lie back. "You sit back now, and let me do all the work."

Oh, hell yeah.

* * *

LATER THAT MORNING, Lexi phoned Jessie and told her she wouldn't be working for the rest of the day.

"I need a break," Lexi explained, knowing Jessie would understand.

"After that scene today, I don't blame you," Jessie said. "I heard Luke was a total hero today. Both Mom and Sabrina couldn't stop talking about how he pulled you all out of there."

"Oh, yeah. That." Not her proudest moment.

"Are you crazy going after Iris like that? She's always stirred up trouble. Do you want to get *everyone* talking again?"

"Sorry. I temporarily lost my mind."

"Mom brings it out of all of us. Good thing Luke was there. Where is he now? Some of his fans are asking. Is he back hiding in his room?"

Lexi cleared her throat. "How should I know where he is?"

Silence from Jessie, then, "He's right there, isn't he?"

Lexi let out a big sigh. "Jessie, would you quit that?"

"Quit what?"

"Reading my mind!" Lexi hissed into the phone. Because seriously, her sister. Damn!

"Sure thing. It's right here on my to-do list. Check with Olga on food supplies right after *stop reading my sister like a paperback novel.* Anyway, rest and relax. Take the rest of the day."

"Thanks. I will." Lexi hung up and stretched out on her tangled sheets.

She was lying completely naked and had been in this marvelous state for hours. She felt decadent and irresponsible, two words which would never be attributed to her before today. Right here on her bed in the middle of the day with a man who had the best hands, the best mouth, the best tongue.

Turned out she wouldn't be getting his Gibson, and quite frankly she was good with that.

No promises.

No regrets.

Yes, sir that was her new modus operandi. Wait, was that modus operanda? Whatever.

Actually, grapes would be good right now. And Luke, feeding them one by one to her. He still had some making up to do. She giggled at the thought, although hey, stranger things had happened. But at the moment, the man with the best of everything was further proving it by strumming on her guitar. He was on the other side of the opened French doors, stretched out on the couch. Half-naked. Making her guitar sing.

Thirty minutes ago, he'd pulled his jeans back on, the top

button undone, no shirt, and cooked for her again. Grilled cheese. A little making out after she'd complimented him on the best grilled cheese sandwiches in all the land, and then he'd made his way to the guitar. Luke could never be away from the guitar for long. Once it had been that way for her. Now she had to force herself to play, knowing if she didn't, she'd get rusty. Lose the finger calluses which had been so hard won.

But the joy and the drive to play and write? That part hadn't been there for a while until recently.

The short story? She'd burned out and knew it. The long story went somewhere along the lines that deep inside that truth was the fear that she'd never have another song come out of her again. No more fruit on the vine. She was a dried-up husk of a songwriter who, at the ripe age of twenty-eight, was already a has-been. That was certainly what the label, and anyone who mattered in country music, believed.

Quit feeling sorry for yourself.

And true enough, why was she lying here all alone when within a few feet of her was her man? The one she'd been apart from too long. She grabbed a long tee shirt and threw it on, then went to join him.

He looked up when he saw her approach, and an easy smile spread across his face and lit up his chocolate eyes. "Hey, baby."

"Don't stop." The couch barely fit two, but she sat and curved her body to his back to save room. "I like to hear you play."

He strummed for a while and then added a melody, plunking it out note by note. "Something new."

She kissed his back, then buried her face in his neck. "It sounds like another winner."

Luke was such a gifted songwriter, though she wasn't sure he understood quite how gifted. Even with all his talent, he'd still seemed shocked that anyone would want to hear him play his own songs. Now he had the success to back it, so she hoped he finally believed in himself as much as she did.

"You're talented, babe." She kissed his shoulder. "Tell me you get that."

He snorted. "Yeah."

She gave his shoulder a love bite. "Don't make me slap you."

"It's a job, baby. And much better than working on the boatyard."

Not quite true. It was a job, like any other, but also a passion. In a relatively short time, Luke had achieved something few in their business could. And as much as she missed him, this was his life now. She'd never take that away from him.

"What's the song called?" she asked.

"Working title? Get Her Back." He didn't look at her, but kept strumming. When she didn't say anything, he added with a smirk, "You know I suck at lyrics. And titles."

And of course, she happened to most assuredly not suck at lyrics or titles. It was her favorite part, the way she could tell a short story in a song. Country music was like that more than any other musical genre.

"If it wasn't for you, *Falling for You* would be a different kind of song," he said.

"What kind would it be?"

"Don't know, maybe about a guy working on his Harley?" He chuckled. "Kidding."

Mad as she'd been with the songs he'd written about their break-up, she was now flattered that he'd care enough to write about missing her. But while her songs told a story, beginning, middle, and end, most of his songs were right in the middle. Which, she had to admit, worked for him.

"Luke, seriously, you can do this. Just start at the beginning and tell a story. We all love stories. What if he's working on his Harley and a beautiful girl drives by? What if he recognizes her because she's got a certain reputation in town? What if he finds out there's more to the story? She's trapped in a loveless marriage. She's abused. She's unloved."

Luke stopped strumming and turned to look at her over his shoulder at her. "Damn, baby. That's depressing."

"Alright, it's not my best idea. I'm just giving you an example."

"No, it was good." His hand came to rest on her knee right behind him and he stroked, causing a shiver to pulse through her leg. "Just sad."

"It's all in the delivery."

When Luke started playing again, Lexi began to hum along, their voices blending together. She then added words, which seemed to just come out of the sky. Straight out of nowhere. Sometimes it happened that way, a song fully formed and needing little or no work, though it hadn't in a long time. Luke followed along, just adding his voice to the harmony as he came to learn the words.

An hour later, they had one verse and the chorus to a brand-new song. Excited, Lexi grabbed paper and a pen and scribbled it all down while Luke smiled at her from under hooded eyelids.

"This is good."

Much better than her sex song that tried too hard. This was her first song without a beginning, middle, and end. This one was right in the middle. This one was simple and beautiful, like a gift. Of course, it was Luke's melody. "I think this might be good."

Luke stopped playing and set the guitar down in its stand. He stood and pulled Lexi up by her elbows. "Try fantastic. Seems like we're still pretty good collaborators. C'mere."

His hands drifted down from the side of her waist, to her hips. Then he hooked a hand under her knee and pulled her leg up around his hip. He kissed her hard and long, and by the time he was done they were both panting. With warm hands squarely on her butt, he lifted her straight into his arms. She wrapped her legs around him tightly, and he carried her back to bed.

CHAPTER 17

"I'm so glad I don't have to hunt for my food. I don't even know where tacos live." ~ Meme

*L*uke spent the night.

In the morning, Lexi slid out from under his arm. She'd let him sleep while she took a shower and got ready for work. She'd had her day off and her fun and self-indulgence. Now it was time to get back to work and her part in the business of running an inn. She made her way to the kitchen to make the coffee, and when she passed the short hallway from the kitchen towards the front room, she peeked in the bedroom to see that Luke had barely stirred. He still had one arm slung over his face, the other stretched out to where she'd slept next to him all night.

Poor guy. He was so not a morning person. She understood. Lexi hadn't been one for years, either, but coffee had changed all that. Now, the best thing about the morning was her first cup of coffee. She liked it dark and rich with exactly three tablespoons of creamer. And she looked forward to it every day as her morning treat. Most of the time, she'd sit on the couch after her shower with a mug of coffee and check email.

She sat on the couch now with her laptop stretched over her thighs to do just that, but curiosity bested her, and she performed a Google search on Luke Wyatt. Now that the man was sacked out only a few feet away from her, she did so for the first time in months, finding it only slightly ironic. Dozens of websites popped up, including his personal website, Twitter with nearly a million followers (she went ahead and followed him), Wikipedia, and Instagram. A few of his song videos were on YouTube. Links to articles about him on Rolling Stone and Billboard. Next, the *people also ask* questions. Among them "who opens for Luke Wyatt," "who writes songs for Luke Wyatt," and "who is Luke Wyatt engaged to?"

Who is Luke Wyatt engaged to.

Lexi clicked the arrow down. The information was reportedly from an article from *Country Star* and it read:

Unconfirmed sources claim that Luke Wyatt is back in his hometown of Whistle Cove, California to plan his wedding to Lexi Wilder, the singer-songwriter formerly of the award- winning, chart-topping Wilder Sisters. The two songwriting partners have been on again, off again for years. Luke's debut song, Falling for Forever, was written with Lexi Wilder and topped the charts at #1 for eight consecutive weeks.

She'd always wondered about these unconfirmed 'sources.' Reports and rumors of their engagement had been going around for years. Luke had always said that he wanted to be the first to know about his engagement. She could be the second. It would have been nice, had the timing been right, but it never had been.

And it still wasn't.

She heard movement and glanced to see him as he rolled over on his side and opened one eye. He had apparently registered that she wasn't in the bed with him and scowled. Either the scowl was because the night had dared to turn into morning, or because she should still be in bed with him.

She smiled at him. "Luke, we're engaged again. Congratulations."

This was such a common private joke between them that she knew he'd get it immediately.

He groaned, and then added, "Come back here."

"Sorry. I've got work to do today."

"Work me," he said, then covered his face with a pillow.

She laughed and checked her email. Not much these days, other than the occasional one from Miranda's people who wanted to know if she had anything to send them yet. In addition, a fledging music school wanted help with fundraising and would love a free concert. She hadn't performed in a year, but that hardly mattered to them. Some days, Lexi didn't even want to look.

Mostly she had a lot of junk mail and one email with subject matter, 'Photos.' Cringing, Lexi shut her eyes as a pinch of unease rolled through her stomach. She assumed it was another email piling on her little sister, or worse asking if she would intervene and get them a one time exclusive.

The email wasn't about Sabrina, but from Jennifer, editor in chief with *Country Star*:

My photographer took these photos without permission. I deeply apologize on her behalf, and she's been disciplined. But since they're so compelling I would love to publish them in our online magazine with your consent and that of Luke's. We've been in touch with his publicist. Our website has approximately 500,000 unique visitors a day. It would go along with a positive and uplifting article on how you and Luke Wilder are together again. Of course, I will wait for your approval. Again, my apologies.

Photos of her and Luke. All taken in the past few days. In one photo, they had just left *The Crow's Nest*. Luke had his hand wrapped around the back of her neck, holding her close, face bent low to hers. They were nearly sharing a breath, and the impression might have been, if any random person were looking, that it was a passionate moment rather than an angry one. Lexi had a hand against his chest and one on his waist, but that was less a romantic gesture from her than one in which she was simply trying to hold him back.

Taking another sip of her coffee, she studied the photo because there was something oddly compelling about it. She didn't know anything about photo composition, but her guess was that this person knew what they were doing. Luke looked his usual badass self, holding on to her like he wouldn't let her go. It was another glimpse of the old Luke. *Her* Luke.

There were other photos, too, not surprisingly of the scene over at Lulu's Day Spa. Luke, stalking towards them, the usual easy smile missing. Another of Luke inside the truck and driving away.

She wasn't surprised this intrusion was starting all over again, this time with her and Luke's personal relationship taking the spotlight. Before he'd branched out on his own, before the gold album where he'd told the world he lost *the* girl, the press hadn't bothered them. No one had questions about the back-up guitar player always seen with Lexi. For a moment, she was back to how she'd felt when Luke first released the album. Violated. A bit of an overreaction she could now freely admit. Now she understood that Luke had wanted her back and told her through his music. He must have known it was the most direct punch to her heart.

But at least the curiosity and intrusions were no longer on Sabrina. Lexi could take the hit into her personal life if it misdirected from someone who'd had enough negative attention to last her a lifetime. She could live with this. It wasn't cruel.

She carried her laptop back to the edge of the bed, sat with crossed legs, and nudged Luke. "Hey."

He rolled to her, lowering the pillow, and gave her a lazy smile. "You're back."

"Bad news. Seems your photographer lady followed us." She pointed to the email. "She took photos of us."

Like he'd just been splashed with ice-cold water, Luke sat up ramrod straight. "What the—" Rubbing his eyes, he took the laptop from her, read the email, and then palmed his face. "Baby."

"They are beautiful photos for the most part, you have to admit."

"I told her you were off limits. That I wouldn't talk about you and me."

"I believe you. But everyone wants a good story."

He hit reply and even with hooded eyes began to hunt and peck. "You shouldn't have to put up with this."

Lexi slapped his hand. "Luke, let's just let them publish the photos. There's no real harm."

He palmed his face. "But this is because of me. You deserve your privacy. I promised when I came here that I'd give you that."

Lexi stared at the photos once more. If not for the fact she'd known they were fighting, she'd have thought they were about to kiss.

"Luke." She tipped his chin to meet her eyes. "It's okay."

He'd brought the press to Whistle Cove as she suspected he would. But he'd also made her life rich and interesting again. Passionate. He'd reminded her of who she was.

"Yeah?" Pushing the laptop aside, he hooked his arm around her and tucked her under him. "You have to show me that you forgive me. That's the only way I'll believe you."

And she did, for the next hour, until it was finally time to get to work.

* * *

LUKE TOOK a jog on the beach to calm the hell down. To wake up. First, it was *morning*. Second, the email. Photos taken without permission, probably with one of those zoom lenses. Others that clearly were taken at the spa day fiasco. Anger and frustration slammed into him. He'd come here to help and not hurt her more. While Lexi would probably continue to refuse his money, instead now she could thank him for a photographer following them around and taking photos without their permission.

Slowing down, he pulled out his phone, and dialed Gary.

He picked up immediately. "Hey, how's the sand and surf in your neck of the woods?"

"Not good." Luke explained the recent email and unauthorized photos from the photographer.

"You've hit the big time, Luke," Gary said. "Are they good photos, at least?"

"Yeah. Lexi liked them."

"Have you responded?"

"Not yet."

"Good. Let me take care of all that."

"Yeah?"

"I'll make sure the article is flattering and positive. Need to earn my keep."

Despite his chest tightening from the level of stress he'd been under, Luke actually chuckled. He let out a breath. For the first time in his life, he didn't have to do everything. He could depend on other people to help. Pride had been in the way of all that before, but pride wasn't going to stand in the way of Lexi's privacy and her safety.

"Appreciate it, bud."

"Say no more. How's the songwriting going?"

He wasn't going to say anything to Gary, but last night, he

was certain that he and Lexi had gold. The song, which would have been a bunch of inane lyrics without her, had turned into something special. Just like her. The lyrics weren't at all like *Falling for You*, but more of a testament to fighting to stay together. He hoped in Lexi's case the song was autobiographical, too. But then again, she'd always been the cause of too much hoping on his part. More than ever before in his sorry life.

But this was all happening too fast for her, and she'd said "no promises." She'd said it, he hadn't. His promise was always going to be to have her back. To keep her safe. Nothing had changed in that regard, other than the fact that he might be able to afford a bodyguard now. But that wasn't him. He took care of his own.

"Don't know, but I think we just might hit country gold again."

"We?"

Luke cleared his throat. "Yeah, me and Lexi."

"Holy shit, dude! You did it."

"It was just a lucky thing. I've written a few songs so far, but this one with her is a cut above."

"Surprised she'd even talk to you, much less write a song with you."

"You don't know her like I do." She'd loved him before he had anything to offer at all.

He didn't want to risk what he had ever again. But there wasn't much time left now, and he would have to pave the road for her to come back to Nashville with him. Soon.

On his way back to his room, he spotted Kit sitting at an inside table with Mrs. Wilder and her Sir. That's right. It was breakfast time, and he was actually awake. Some coffee might even improve on that. He headed up to his room to shower and change and was back before the Wilder family reunion had ended.

He headed to the buffet to load up, trying to ignore the giggles he heard from some of the women in line. "Mornin,'" he said to a woman who angled near him and bumped his elbow.

"You eat breakfast!" she said. "That's *so* awesome!"

"Thanks," he mumbled, "Maybe I'll get an award for it at this year's CMA."

That was apparently the funniest thing anyone had ever heard. The woman and her friend both laughed and asked if they might get his autograph after he was done eating. He agreed, and trying hard not to look at anyone, he started back to his room when he heard the distinct voice of Kit calling.

"Luke." She stood and waved. "Over here!"

He supposed this was at least better than eating alone having strangers watch him chew, and might give him a chance to talk to Kit about how to get Lexi's career back on track. So, though he had planned on taking his food back to the pink room, he turned and walked toward the Wilders.

"Sit with us," Kit said, and gestured to Mrs. Wilder and Sir Clint. "This is Clint. I'm not kidding. *Clint.*"

"We've met," Luke said as he took a seat across from Kit.

"How are you, son?" Sir Clint asked. "Did you try the blueberry scones as I advised?"

"I did. You weren't lying." He grinned.

"We were just discussing our day," Mrs. Wilder said.

Kit sighed loudly and tossed her cloth napkin on the table. "I'd be thrilled to plan my day, but first I need to find a room."

"Kit—" Mrs. Wilder began.

"You don't have a room?" Luke said.

"I'm staying with Sabrina, but hoo boy my daughter is messy. And besides, we're both a bit of a clotheshorse so I need some more room."

"Apparently you're the cause of zero vacancy," Clint said. "My congratulations to you."

"We appreciate your staying here." Mrs. Wilder added.

"It's not a problem." Luke leaned back in his chair, trying to gracefully accept all the gratitude he didn't deserve. He'd come for Lexi but if he'd been able to help the B&B in the process, it was extra.

"Yes, thank you, Luke," Kit said as almost an afterthought. "It's just what the B&B needed. I had no idea we were struggling so much."

Luke noted the "we" though he had the distinct impression that Kit had never been much involved much with the Wilder Sisters B&B.

"Have to admit," Luke said, daring to look past his tablemates, and finding too many open-mouthed looks in his direction. "It's a little…distracting."

"Yes," Kit said. "You all never stopped to think of what this might do to Luke's creative well. Too many fans insisting on his attention when he should be writing."

"Oh, I'm so sorry," Mrs. Wilder, the kindest woman Luke had ever met, said. "I'm sure we didn't mean—"

"Don't worry. I'm hanging out in my room, mostly," Luke said. "And getting a lot of writing done."

"Which room is that?" Kit asked.

"The…pink one."

Kit laughed. "The Mermaid Room. My favorite. How on earth did you wind up in there?"

"I understand he got moved when he extended his stay because the Captain's Room had been booked in advance," Mrs. Wilder said.

Luke nodded, remembering fondly how he'd stayed not just because he wanted to, but because Lexi admitted she needed him. "That's right."

"The Mermaid Room is hardly the right room for you," Kit said. "Maybe we could move you."

"He's already been moved once," Mrs. Wilder said. "I'd hate to do that to him. Besides, we're booked now. It's the reason *you* can't have a room."

"Yes, you're right. You're right. What to do? What to do?" Kit put her chin in her hand and looked wistfully to the crashing waves in the distance.

He knew exactly what she wanted. "You can have my room, Kit."

"What?" Mrs. Wilder said.

"Son—" Clint started.

"I'll still pay for it. I don't mean that," Luke said. This was one way he could help financially, and Lexi would be none the wiser. "Truth is the pink isn't my thing."

"But where will you stay?" Mrs. Wilder said. "Somewhere in town?"

"I'll figure something out. Maybe I'll camp out on the beach." At Mrs. Wilder's horrified expression, he added, "Kidding."

"I don't want to put you out," Kit said.

She did, but no matter. "No problem."

"If you insist," Kit said, ending the discussion. "That's kind of you."

"Yes, it is," Clint said. "You're a gentleman."

Yeah, he was such a great guy. He had to agree. Had just managed to get himself kicked out of the only room available, so that now he'd have to stay with Lexi. Too bad. A few minutes and some small talk later, Mrs. Wilder and Clint excused themselves. They had plans for the day. Kit, of course, stayed. Luke was not surprised.

Sabrina approached from a table where she'd been chatting with guests and refreshing their coffee. "Good morning, two of my favorite people. Coffee?"

"No, thanks." Luke covered his mug. "I'm good."

"Yes, honey. Thanks. You look so pretty today," Kit said, beaming.

"Thanks, Momma. I haven't worn this old thing in ages." Sabrina poured coffee and turned to stage whisper to Luke. "You're biggest fan is at the table behind us. Two from that, is your next biggest fan. And three from that, watch your step. Shark territory and infested waters."

"Good to know." Once again, the Wilder sisters all had his back. His second family.

Once Sabrina was off, Kit turned to Luke, all pretense dropped. He could see it in her crazy-chick eyes. She was three-fourths of the way to her Grand Plan, coming in hot. And he was going to help her.

"Can I be honest?" Kit said.

"Yep."

"Whether you and Lexi reconcile or not, I think you and I both agree that she belongs back in Nashville. On the road and in a recording studio. Singing, performing, and writing songs. *Not* running a B&B."

"Agreed."

"So…I can count on you? To put in a good word with the powers that be, to get Lexi back on track with her music?"

He leaned back in his seat. "Kit, far as I'm concerned, I'll take her back to Nashville with me, kicking and screaming all the way. It just would be much better if she agreed it's where she belongs. It would make for an easier plane ride. Kidding about the kicking and screaming, of course."

She winked. "Sounds like we both have our work cut out for us."

While he didn't necessarily like having Kit for a partner, he worked with what he had. Always had. He, more than most people, understood that partnerships were at times formed out of mutual need more than respect. But he did respect Kit, first and foremost, because say whatever else you could say about her (and there was plenty he *could* say, much of it not nice) she loved her daughters. Wanted the best for them. She loved Lexi. He loved Lexi.

They had a common purpose.

Bringing her home.

CHAPTER 18

"You can't always control who walks into your life, but you can control which window you throw them out of." ~ Meme

At the end of the day, Lexi only wanted a guitar in her arms. The song with Luke had fired her up. She'd spent the rest of her day making up songs while she worked. Songs about colorful towels. Songs about blue sheets. A song about Olga and Tony, which caused the cook to laugh at Lexi in delight. There were songs about some of the most interesting guests at the B&B. She imagined that an older couple she'd spied walking along the beach during her break had a long history. They'd come to the B&B to re-awaken what they'd had once. It was their last chance. That song she'd titled, *Last Chance Hotel*, but it was too short.

It was as if she was twelve again, writing songs on the way to school and singing them to her sisters in the evening. Either way, her creativity had definitely been split wide open. None of these songs and lyrics was anything she could use, but at least she was on to something more. Something better. It was exciting to feel the inspiration punching through her spirit again, with actual enjoyment instead of the overwhelming and intense pressure to perform. To sell.

She fairly danced her way to her cottage, but when she opened the door, there was Luke sitting on her couch, playing his Gibson. She stopped in her tracks, simply admiring how wonderful he looked decorating her couch. How nice of him. The muscles of his forearms bunched as his arm worked up and down the neck of the guitar. The smile he slid her was easy. Slow. Sexy.

"Your mom wants the pink room." His fingers continued through a chord progression. "I let her have it."

"You...you did?" Her skin tightened with that wonderful feeling of desire and deep affection.

"Yeah, I was a real nice guy. A gentleman, Sir Clint said. That's high praise coming from him. Imagine me, a *gentle*man." He stopped playing and set the guitar to the side.

She was still rooted to her spot by the door, wondering how her mother had managed this feat. The woman had talent, she'd say that. Luke had never been crazy about her, and so he wasn't likely to indulge her.

"She has an ulterior motive. She just wants us to get back together, so you can help my career. That's all."

"Yeah, and I'm okay with it." He stood.

"But—" She'd been about to say that Kit's purpose was wrong and self-serving, and that she'd simply tried to use Luke to get what she wanted. She'd never wanted him for Lexi until he'd made such a monumental success of himself. He had to know that. She didn't want to say it out loud and hurt his feelings.

"Hey, turns out there's a first time for everything." He simply stood, hands in the pockets of his faded low-rise jeans, rocking back on his heels. "Your mother and I on the same side."

Lexi didn't like Mom using Luke as if she had any right

to. And she didn't like either *one* of them conspiring together, for whatever purpose they were conspiring together. *She* would be the one to make the decisions in her life from now on. For years, she'd had no choice. Now she did. This was something she'd need to explain to both her mother and Luke. There would be no more managing Lexi Wilder. She'd manage herself, thank you very much.

It didn't change the fact that he made her bones liquid just by giving her a simple crooked smile.

"Lex?" he said, cocking his head. "You still with me?"

Something loosened inside. Something crazy. Irrational and yeah, just a little buck wild. She took two steps and launched herself into his arms. Fortunately, he'd braced for her the moment he'd seen her coming and caught her easily. He had one arm tight around her waist, and lowered the other one to her butt.

She buried her face in his neck, taking in a long deep breath of his earthy, beachy, and one hundred percent male scent. "Here I am."

"Here you are, baby." His lips trailed a line of wet, hot kisses down her neck as he moved through the French doors to the bedroom.

He threw her on the bed and began divesting her of her clothes quicker than she'd believed possible. Shirt, bra, jeans, and panties took flight. Then again, he was always a bit of a magician that way. She helped pull his shirt off, and the rest followed. Quickly. They both worked fast, their breaths coming shallow and ragged. She wasn't interested in tender and slow. He seemed to agree this time, his kisses coming faster, deeper, and more desperate. For her part, she clawed at his back, trying to pull him closer.

They'd used protection for years, but she didn't think about it now as Luke moved swiftly inside her with one powerful thrust. Then, he moved fast, his strokes steady and deeper each time. Lexi threw her head back as the intense pressure rose inside of her. When Luke hooked his arm under her knee and pulled up, he went deeper still. She lost her mind, grazing her teeth along his shoulder. Coming closer and closer to that peak where she'd lose herself. Where she didn't know where she ended, and he began.

The pulsating waves of pressure built deep inside her, pressing down and radiating through her body. Spreading like wildfire in her blood. When she couldn't contain it any longer, she cried out, her body shaking and convulsing. He followed her a moment later, and by the way he did, she could tell he'd been holding back and simply waiting for her. Even here, even when it was fast, he always took care of her.

"Baby," Luke groaned into her mouth. "Are you trying to kill me?"

Breaths still coming slow and thin, Lexi framed his face. "Did... I... tell you that I missed you?"

His lips twitched. "No, but I think you just did."

"Right. Boy, did I miss you."

"Right back at ya." He rolled on his back, taking her with him and tucking her into his side. "You won't have to miss me again. If you come with me to Nashville."

And there it was. Her body became one tight coil, and she moved, trying to pull away from him. But he only tightened his hold.

"We said no promises."

"You said that. I didn't." He buried his face in her hair, and she heard his somewhat muffled voice. "I have only one promise to make. Never take you for granted again."

"Luke—"

"No, don't argue with me. I love you, and I always thought I'd have you by my side. It was a mistake to assume that."

She felt the fresh salty wetness of tears. It was too soon to think about all this. She'd wanted to enjoy his last week here with him without thoughts of wondering what would happen when he left. How she'd feel when he left. Life was too short, and there was plenty of time to be sad and depressed.

Such as after he left, and she stayed.

When she didn't respond but simply sniffled into his neck, he pulled her back by the nape of her neck. "Can you tell me you don't love me anymore?"

In all honesty, she couldn't say those words. If she did, she'd be lying. She might get away with that for a short time, but to what end? He'd see right through her.

"I…can't say that."

His lopsided grin took that in for a minute. "So, you love me?"

"I do, you idiot." She finger-thumped his chest. "But it's not that easy. I've started a life here. My sisters are here, and they need me. Especially Sabrina. Gran needs me, and the B&B needs me."

"And I need you."

Her heart tugged at the romance behind those four words. "But you're a big guy, and you'll be alright without me."

"No, I won't." His hands tightened around her.

"There's always…long distance." But she knew that would never work. It hadn't worked.

"We already tried that."

She sighed because he was right. With the pressures of fame and the road, of Nashville and all its many intricacies, being apart wouldn't work. Not for long.

"I don't want to talk about it now." She nestled further into his arms, lowering her head to kiss one solid pec. "There are other things we could be doing, and we're wasting time."

He chuckled, then in one swift move pinned her under him. "Tell me again."

Of course, she knew exactly what he wanted to hear. But giving it to him immediately would be far too easy. Did she mention how much she loved teasing him? "I said there are other things we could be doing."

"Yeah, not that." He pressed into her. "Tell me."

"We're wasting time?" She batted her eyelashes.

"Try again." He gazed at her from underneath his lashes. "Tell me."

Because she'd tortured him enough in the past week, she threaded her fingers around his neck and tugged him close enough to share a single breath. "I love you, Luke."

"Yeah?" He smiled with satisfaction, dark eyes shimmering. "I know it. Love you too, baby."

And for the next few hours, he proceeded to show it...very well.

CHAPTER 19

"The only kind of exercise I get is jumping to conclusions."~ Meme

The next few days passed in a haze of sex, music, work, and also more sex, with occasional breaks for sleeping, eating, and sex. Lexi spent her nights with Luke and her days trying to get something else done. Luke was still writing, doing phone interviews with Nashville and local radio stations, and any press he could manage long distance. She was still folding towels and sheets while writing songs, visiting Olga in the kitchen and Jessie in the office. And mostly avoiding Mom, who was spending her time taking care of Sabrina, taking her away from what little she did do around here.

Soon enough, Lexi would have to think about Luke going back to Nashville, but for now she simply refused to contemplate it. This was easy enough to do since every time she thought of him leaving, her throat closed up. A pebble that was much more like a boulder lodged in her throat. She'd chosen instead to simply enjoy him. Enjoy the way he made such male sounds, his voice rough and rumbling in her ear talking dirty. His beard, a delectable combination of rough and soft on every part of her naked and exposed body. She enjoyed the tightness in his shoulders when he worked to hold back his own orgasm longer. When he told her he loved her over and over again. When he crawled up her body.

Lexi was simply grateful that her mother had stayed out of her and Luke's way and hadn't pressed her about leaving for Nashville with him. Lexi was in a tough enough position without the added stress from Mom. Half of Lexi couldn't see staying in Whistle Cove without Luke. The other half couldn't see leaving her sisters behind.

For so long, they'd been the three musketeers. Just the three of them, holding each other up and having each other's backs. How could she have their backs all the way from Nashville? How could she possibly have a career without Sabrina and Jessie at her side? Even if Sabrina had given Lexi the green light to go ahead, that wouldn't make this any easier. Jessie would be fine because she enjoyed her work at the B&B, was good at it, and never had the same passion for music that Sabrina and Lexi did. But Sabrina. She'd never be able to work at the B&B long-term. It would be like trapping a firefly under a basket.

Lexi had to fix that and so many other things. And as Luke frequently reminded her, she had to think of him, too, because that's what people who loved each other did. And she did love him. Too much sometimes. She was pretty sure he'd disagree there was such a thing as loving him too much, but what could she call it when she'd almost be willing to give up her own happiness for his? Too much love, that's what.

She was on her way to the weekly meeting with Jessie when she overheard her saying, "Enjoy your stay."

"I'm sure I will," a man said with a deep southern drawl.

Lexi watched the man walk away. He wore a tight pair of

Wranglers with a large silver belt buckle and a black Stetson. Old school country. The man was none other than Gary, Luke's manager. Lexi ducked into the office, so as not to be forced to say hello to him. She hadn't had enough coffee for Gary. She wasn't sure there *was* enough.

"I thought we didn't have any vacancy," Lexi said when Jessie joined her in the office. How had Gary managed to get a room? Connections? Luke?

"Well, there have been some cancellations since you and Luke…" Jessie said. "Um, made it so…obvious?"

It was true. Obvious was their ship name. Forget Luxe or Luxie for a combo name. They were Captain Obvious, both of them. They'd often walk hand in hand along the private beach together, sit side by side in the Adirondack chairs, play guitar, and make out a little when they thought no one else was watching.

Which was probably never.

And Lexi had noticed the sudden lack of beautiful women and the resurgence of couples. "Oh, great. I'm sorry, Jess. I should have…I didn't think—"

Jessie held up a palm. "Don't be ridiculous. Like you're supposed to stop loving him to save our business? No one thinks that. Luke helped us out of a slump."

"We're still doing better?"

"Funny thing is, once we had a waiting list, we had our target guests interested again. And that's probably simply because we *had* a wait list."

"Ah. Catch-22. No one wants to visit until they *can't*."

"I can't tell you how happy they are to be called when we have an opening."

"And Gary? What's he doing here?"

"He said he was meeting Luke." Jessie glanced at Lexi, eyebrows knotted. "He didn't mention it?"

"No."

She *wouldn't* panic or jump to conclusions. Luke must have had a good reason not to mention it. Either Luke didn't know, which probably wasn't likely, or he hadn't wanted to tell her that he was bringing Nashville to her own backyard. She understood why. He'd be afraid she'd make too much out of it, for one. Already Lexi's palms were sweaty and her throat closing up. Next, her stomach would follow, dropping like a stock market crash. Singing and playing again was one thing, but she still felt skittish about the business. The record company executives, handlers, and all the rest who often made decisions about an artist's life.

"Are you thinking about going back to Nashville with him?" Jessie asked.

"Don't worry about that," Lexi said, waving her hand dismissively.

"I do worry," Jessie said.

"Well, you shouldn't. I'm never going to leave you hanging. You should know that. It's the Wilder Sisters together forever." She leaned forward and fist bumped with Jessie.

"That's not what I'm worried about."

"Sabrina? She'll be fine. Sure, we've got to work on her, and we've got our work cut out for us, but let's wait until Mom goes back."

"Lexi—"

"I've got a few things in mind. For instance, a comeback for Sabrina. We both know that's what she wants. But the timing has to be right. I think—"

"Lexi!" Jessie shouted.

"What?" Irritated, Lexi stopped cold and stared at her sister.

Her middle sister. The peacemaker of the family. The solid foundation of the sisters. And she looked pretty pissy right now. Her lips were straight, eyebrows lowered. Eyes squinting.

"It's time you get a clue. You've *got* to go back with him."

"No. No, I don't. I have to stay here with you. And Sabrina needs me, let's face it. How would she take it if I just pick up and went back to Nashville, leaving her behind?"

"She'll be fine. After all, she can visit you. Eventually. We all can. But you, Lex, have been in love with the same man for years. You're good for him. And he's good for you. Once, he fit into your life. Touring with us as a family, sharing you with all of us, and our fans. Now it's time you fit into *his* life."

"It's not that easy."

"It should be."

Lexi pushed back tears. Jessie holding down the fort with Sabrina? What if they needed her? What if something worse than a sprained knee happened to her Gram? "But I... I don't want to leave you."

"I'm going to miss you, but it was going to happen sooner or later. Someday, I realized a long time ago, one of us would get married. Be the first to start a family. Start a new offshoot of the Wilder sisters. Who knows? Maybe the Wyatt sisters. You and Luke might have daughters someday."

"I'm not ready for that!"

"Then go with him and take it one step at a time. But you *have* to go with him. There's no other way. I will personally kick your ass if you blow this. He's the best thing that ever happened to you. *And* you love him."

"I wish we could all go together." Because she did love Luke, and the time apart had shown her how much she didn't want to live without him. She could and she had. Now it was a choice.

"No, you don't really want that." Jessie smiled. "But I promise you, I'll hold down the fort. Take care of Gran and the B&B. Take care of Sabrina. For once, I want you to take care of yourself."

It was exactly what she thought she'd been doing here all

along. Taking care of herself. Taking a long break from her old life. The world she'd grown up in, the one in which she'd been a responsible twelve-year-old, writing songs and performing while going to school. It had been the life of a grown up early on. So, she'd taken a break from responsibilities. From everything. But then Luke had shown up with his Gibson, his beard, and his crooked smile. Reminding her of what she'd lost. Once the taste of playing and writing was back in her blood again, it had been impossible to let it go. She wanted music in her life again almost as much as she wanted Luke. But this time, she wouldn't compromise her personal life and happiness for it.

"Isn't that being selfish?"

"No, it's not. You're the least selfish person I know. This is called living your life. And you can't stay stuck forever. You and I both know this isn't where you belong. Not anymore."

"Jess," Lexi said, her eyes suddenly watery. "I'm going to miss you so much."

Jessie stood up and walked around the desk to pull Lexi into a hug. "Me too."

"Everyone's going with me to the airport and straight through TSA to wait with me."

"I don't know if they allow that, but if we have to huddle at the line we'll do that until they peel us off you."

"You're going to visit me all the time," Lexi said.

"And Skype, too. You're going to get so sick of me."

After her talk with Jessie, Lexi went to work where she was needed. Today it was with Olga in the kitchen, helping to set up the buffet and serve the hot dish. A crispy bacon, egg, cheese and potato dish. Stepping behind Olga, Lexi grabbed her in a fierce hug. She was going to miss so much about Whistle Cove and her family here.

"What's wrong?" Olga turned to face Lexi.

"Nothing. You're the sweetest woman on earth, you know that?"

"Oh, mi hijita. Did you spill some of the dish? It's okay, we've got plenty."

"No." Lexi laughed. "Have you ever been to Nashville?"

Olga smiled and swatted Lexi's shoulder. "You know I haven't."

"You'll have to come and visit me. And Luke."

The light in Olga's eyes changed from curiosity to a twinge of sadness. "You've leaving us again."

"I'll be back to visit."

"I know you will. And we will visit you." She planted a kiss on Lexi's cheek.

"You better."

Because, God help her, she was going with Luke. It didn't mean she'd made a decision about her career yet. She'd simply made a decision about her heart. And she couldn't live without Luke. He would be her family now.

Jessie was right. It was time to be her own person and separate from her sisters. They'd always be sisters, but they'd never be performing sisters again. Never live together again, or be involved in every single aspect of each other's lives. And that was okay. Slowly, she would say her goodbyes to everyone this week, leaving her sisters for last. It would by far be the hardest goodbye.

Lexi found Gran on one of the roomy cushioned couches in the room they used for wine tasting hour. She had her leg with the bad ankle resting on the matching ottoman. A book in her hands. *Wuthering Heights.*

"I need to talk to you." Lexi took a seat next to her. "It's important."

Gran simply turned to her, misty gray eyes calm and steady.

"I'm going back to Nashville with Luke. I didn't think I

would, but then Luke said…and Sabrina and Jessie said…and so…but I *know*. This is what I want. To be with him."

Gran closed her book. "Honey, I'm glad. John believed you had a gift, and you do. But it's definitely not running a B&B."

"Hey, I thought I was going okay." Lexi elbowed her.

"Sure, honey, but remember last week when you thought I bought new pink towels?"

"Yeah?"

"You're not supposed to combine red and white in the wash. They turned pink."

"Those pink towels were the white towels?" She had wondered where the white towels had gone, but who had time to inventory towels? "Why didn't anyone tell me?"

"I didn't want to hurt your feelings. You tried so hard." Gran put a hand on Lexi's knee. "I'm glad you're going with him. Life is too short. Better hurry with that wedding I know is coming, or I might beat you to it."

"You and Sir Clint?"

"Don't look so shocked. I'm seventy-eight, not dead." She winked.

"If you ever need me here again, I don't want you to hesitate asking. I'll drop everything and come to you."

"I know you will, sweetheart. But we're going to be okay here, Jessie, Sabrina, and me. We may not be sisters, but we're Wilders. And we Wilders always find a way."

After a few more minutes of talking to Gran, in which Lexi learned that she'd accidentally been short-sheeting most of the guest's beds, she left her to check on whether the Captain's Room guests required new towels. She saw Gary out on the deck, and he wasn't alone. Mom was with him, and they were sort of huddled together. Gary nodded, put his hand on her shoulder and patted. She shook her head a couple of times, then gave him a dazzling smile.

She might be talking to Gary about resuscitating Sabrina's career next. That made sense, and a tingle of excitement punched through Lexi as she pictured a not-too-distant future in which Sabrina would be visiting Nashville recording the songs Lexi planned to write for her. She stepped outside to welcome Gary and help him find Luke, who should still be in her bed. It was nine in the morning, and a little on the early side for him.

"...with those two together again, we're sure to hit country gold," Gary was saying.

"I'm so glad you were able to come out. Lexi just needs to hear it from you," Kit said. "It's time she gets back to her music where she belongs. I've already discussed it with Luke, and he agrees."

"Luke came here to write songs and get some inspiration. He needs to follow up that debut album with something big. I knew that writing with Lexi was what he wanted, but I have to admit, I never imagined she would write with him again. He's one silver-tongued devil, let me tell you. Because believe me, whatever it is they wrote together, and Luke told me it's good, it's sure to be a hit."

"My daughter is a gifted songwriter," Kit sniffed. "Her father said so from the start."

"Of course, she is," Gary said, "And we'd be happy to have her on board writing more songs for Luke."

Writing songs for Luke.

Lexi left before she had to listen to another word. She ran down the deck steps, straight for her private stretch of beach where she could think. Where she could scream. God, she was so stupid. Naïve. She hadn't wanted to be right about this, so she'd ignored all the signs. He needed new material, and he'd come to get it. Luke loved her alright.

He loved her songs.

He needed her words.

He wanted more country gold.

Not her.

* * *

LUKE HAD JUST HOPPED out of the shower when he heard pounding on the front door. What was it about people banging on his door when he was naked and wet? He'd stayed here with Lexi for almost a week, but no one had bothered them before. No more photographers or fans snooping around. Even her sisters were staying away. Frankly, he appreciated it more than he had words. For years, he'd shared Lexi with her sisters.

Close as the sisters were, that had been the way she came. Matching baggage in the form of Jessie and Sabrina, with whom she'd shared more than a home most of her adult life. But now, he'd had her all to himself. No tour bus filled with other people. And it could be this way from now on if she came back to Nashville. She could always have her sisters visit them. They'd come back to Whistle Cove often. Point being, he had her back in his arms, in his bed, and he wasn't ever going to let her go again.

"Hang on, I'm coming." Luke dried off quickly, pulled on a pair of jeans commando and opened the door to Gary. Shock rolled through him. "What the hell are *you* doing here?"

Gary dropped on the couch. "Kit invited me, and I thought I'd come check up on you. She said she wanted me to see Lexi and Sabrina too, get reacquainted, and see how I can help their careers. She said the two of you had talked about it, that you were on board with getting Lexi back to Nashville where she belongs."

"That's true, but I'm working on that, and I don't need your help, or Kit's."

Luke had a bad feeling. He shouldn't have been surprised

that a partnership with Kit would somehow come back to blow up in his face. Lexi was used to her mother trying to make alliances with everyone in her circle, and outside of it. Even Lexi could see what she was up to, showing up while Luke was in town and trying to throw them together. Now Gary was here, a firm reminder of Nashville. Lexi wouldn't like any of this.

Worse, she might blame him for it.

He had to quickly find Lexi and explain he'd had nothing to do with Gary's arrival.

"Damn it, Gary. You have the world's worst timing."

CHAPTER 20

"The more you weigh, the harder you are to kidnap. Stay safe. Eat cake."~ Meme

*L*exi jogged as far and as fast as her legs would take her. Past their private access beach to the public one. She ran, causing groups of Seagulls and Pelicans to take flight. She caught the attention of joggers, who did this kind of thing for fun. They smiled and nodded her way. She tried to breathe. In through the nose, out through the mouth. In through the nose...

He's going to need to follow up that debut album with something big.

Didn't think she'd ever write with him again.

He's one silver tongued devil.

Country Gold.

She should have seen it coming. Was that all anyone in Nashville *cared* about? What about family? What about relationships? What about love? What about her? Was that all she had to offer the world? A song?

She stopped, bending over with a stitch in her side. "No!"

she shouted to the crashing ocean waves. "It's not all! I'm a good woman, and I have a lot to offer. Love, friendship, honesty, and loyalty, in case anyone still cares about that kind of thing!"

"Preach!" A fellow jogger said as she moved past Lexi with a hearty wave.

"Uh-huh. That's right." She was still rubbing her side when Luke came running behind her not even slightly out of breath.

"Lexi. Been looking for you. Gary is here."

"I know." She whipped around to face him. "What do *you* want? More country gold?"

"Lex—"

"Because I'm fresh out! Try me back next week when I have a going out of business sale. Everything, half off!" She stalked away.

"Baby, don't you walk away from me."

She stopped and turned to give him the evilest eye she'd ever given anyone. Ever. It was all malevolent and witchy, her right eye twitching and watering. "Watch me do it."

She hadn't taken two steps before he had his arms around her waist, stopping her forward momentum. Head bent, he buried his face in her neck.

Her body betrayed her by responding with a shiver. "Luke! Let me go."

"Not until we talk. Not until you tell me what's wrong."

"I don't want to talk," Lexi said. "I want to run."

"You hate running."

"I'm thinking of taking it up." She pulled, but it was useless.

He turned her in his arms, forcing her to face him. "Tell me."

"I heard Gary and my mother talking. You can drop the 'I love you' act. All any of you want is to bleed me dry. Another hit song. Another city. Another performance. I thought it was different with you, but you came back here for a song. Not for me!"

"No. You got that wrong." Tipping her chin, he whispered, "Want to ask you something. Do you think I'd come here, have you treat me like a leper, put me through my paces, and torture me, just for a song?"

"Whatever you came here for, you got yourself a song. There you go. Maybe that's what we do together best."

"You don't believe that."

"Take the song. I hope we hit the charts again. We could use the money around here."

"I'll never record the song." He pulled her to him. "I don't want the damn song. For me, you're the song."

"Oh, that's good, Luke. See? You can write good lyrics. Now leave me alone like I asked you to do in the first place." She tugged her arm from his reach with no luck.

"No," he said, holding tight to her. "I can't. Not until you talk to me."

"I can't do this with you," Lexi said, wiggling with all her might.

He pressed his forehead to hers with a tight grip on the nape of her neck. Just as he'd done in the parking lot a couple of weeks ago when some creep had taken the photo of them. It was passionate and bold. Like Luke. She started to melt a little bit. This time when her hand went to fist his shirt it wasn't to push him away. It was to get him closer.

"Everything okay here, lady?"

Lexi turned to see a stocky man who looked like he'd just gotten off his job on the docks and pounded back a few. In fact, in his hands, he held a half-empty beer bottle. At nine in the morning.

"I'm—" Lexi said, her palm resting on Luke's chest.

The guy's tone had an edge to it, and he stared at Luke

with a sneer. "Because it looks like Reggie's boy is bothering you."

Lexi's heart kicked up, and her mouth went dry. One of Reggie's friends.

"Walk away," Luke said to the man with equal edge in his tone.

She'd never before heard him sound anything like Reggie's son. Maybe because Luke had worked hard to distance himself from that old life, from where he'd come and his tough beginnings, and he had. But it was still a part of him in some small way. He was still tough and hard and would protect himself and those he loved at all costs.

The man dropped his beer bottle and wiped his chin. "You're a prissy country singer now. But your father never hears from you because you forgot where you came from."

"I didn't forget where I came from," Luke said fiercely, releasing her. His hands turned into fists.

Lexi held on to Luke's arm. "We were having a family fight. A disagreement. I'm okay."

"Too bad I don't believe you," the man said, grabbing Lexi's arm. "Don't worry, honey, I'll show you how a real man treats his woman."

Lexi winced in pain, from both his grab and his words. Cliché much? And oh my God, was she in the middle of a song? If so, this guy was a lousy songwriter. She and Luke could write him under a bus any day of the week without even trying.

"If you want to keep that arm, you better take it off her," Luke threatened.

He sounded so angry, even she'd do whatever he asked right now. She hoped this man would come to his senses, and fast. But it wasn't to be, because in the next moment, the man shoved Lexi aside and went for Luke's throat. He was slightly taller than Luke and certainly had at least twenty pounds on him. Lexi watched as the two men wrestled, Luke gaining the upper hand, but not before he took a fist to his face.

"Stop!" Lexi screamed.

A couple of joggers stood by watching, but didn't seem to know what to do.

"What's going on?" one asked.

"Fight, you idiot," another said.

"That's...not cool."

"Yeah, no kidding."

More observers stopped, expressing concern, but doing exactly nothing. They pulled their phones out and started to record. It was as if they all wished they had a big bag of popcorn with them. Tired of watching this idiot man fight with Luke, Lexi jumped on his back with a loud banshee scream.

It was exactly what she'd wanted to do last week when she'd come between Sabrina and Iris in front of Lulu's Day Spa. The truth was that people were really beginning to piss her off. Luke had done nothing to offend this man, but simply breathe the same air everyone else did and testify against his father. He'd done the heroic thing. The right thing. That was a great offense to this man.

Well, guess what. She was offended too. Offended by people who made rash judgments without understanding the entire situation. This being a perfect example. Another one, Sabrina's indiscretion. She was stupid and naïve but not any of the other nasty names she'd been called. While Lexi clung to the big guy's back, she let her anger take center stage. Her fury was so vicious and real that she knew it wasn't about this man. The anger that raged inside her was against all the record company executives who had cut them loose without a second thought, and all the folks in Nashville who only loved you when you were on top.

"Get off my man!" Lexi screamed, arms wrapped around his neck and squeezing.

But because the man had almost had no neck, it didn't seem to have much of an effect, and instead he shook her off. Lexi went flying off him, landing on her back. She wasn't going to lie. That hurt. She groaned in pain. Unfortunately, this lit a fire in Luke, and he went after the man harder, pinning him and punching with his fists. One after another.

"Stop," Lexi whispered. "Baby, stop."

Luke looked so crazed, so angry, that he might actually hurt the man. That would not be good for anyone, least of all the blockhead. Lexi now considered jumping on Luke's back. Anything to make him stop. But finally, finally, someone intervened. Two male joggers pried Luke off the big guy before he could do any more damage.

And that's when the cops showed up.

It took seeing Luke in the back of a police car for Lexi to understand, for the second time in her life, how quickly some things could spin out of control. The blockhead was in another unit, complaining the cuffs were too tight. He'd blown the breathalyzer and was under arrest for public intoxication and drinking on a public beach. As suspected, he knew Reggie and still worked the docks. He thought Luke was a traitor for turning against his father.

Luke sat in the back of the police car, head down. Officer Drake wouldn't let Lexi near him until he took everyone's statements. Lexi's would be the most important. Only she had seen the man throw the first punch. Everyone else had just seen two men fighting and had witnessed the dolt throw Lexi off his back.

"Can't I please see him?" Lexi begged Drake.

"Tell me what happened first."

Lexi explained it all in a big rush of words. By the time she was done, the officer simply quirked a brow, looking quite amused with her explanation of jumping on the man's back and being thrown off.

"Would you like to press charges?"

"What? No! You're not hearing me. Luke didn't do anything wrong. Anything."

"Ma'am," he said looking at the sky with great patience, "Would you like to press charges against the *other* man? The one sitting in cuffs?"

"No, oh, no. That's...that's okay."

The guy had enough problems without her adding to them. And it wasn't as if she was seriously hurt or anything. Because of Luke, of course. He'd protected her. *My man.* It had been a long time since she'd called him that, but it was true again. He was hers, and she was his. He always would be. Complicated, yes. It would probably would stay that way, too. They both lived in a pressure cooker so it was only natural that some steam would be released on occasion.

"Okay, we're done here," Drake said.

"What about Luke?"

He strode to the back of his cruiser and opened the door. "Do *you* want to press charges?"

Luke had a bloody lip and a bruised eye. He'd looked better, but he didn't seem at all traumatized. "Hell, no."

"Then you're free to go." Drake waved him out.

"You're hurt." Lexi ducked under the officer and crawled into Luke's lap in the back seat of the cruiser.

"I'm fine," Luke said, chuckling. "It's been a long time since I had to kick someone's ass, and it felt damn good."

"You have a bloody lip." She kissed the side of his mouth. She kissed his bruised cheek and eye too.

Luke didn't say anything but groaned softly and started to hum *Cop Car*. And of course, she joined in with a nice harmony for about two seconds before being rudely interrupted.

"Excuse me, but do you two mind getting out of my car?" Drake said. "Now."

"Don't have to ask me twice." Luke picked her up by the waist and set her outside the cruiser, then followed her out.

"I bet you don't have to say *that* to many people," Lexi said to Officer Drake.

"You'll both have to come by the police station later to give your statements," Drake said.

Shaken but not stirred, Lexi walked back to the B&B with Luke, both arms wound tightly around his waist, her face turned into his chest. He'd pulled her in tight, his arm draped around her shoulder. That made moving difficult, but she didn't care. They headed toward her cottage, not speaking. Lexi figured the talking would come later. She'd been so mad, but that was before she'd realized that he'd do anything for her. Even get in a physical fight that might have cost him a lot more than a bruised lip and a black eye.

Luke opened the door and waited for Lexi to walk inside.

Gary, who had been sitting on the couch, shot straight up. "What the hell? Are you okay? Who do I need to call?"

"I'm fine," Luke reiterated.

That should be his catch phrase. Luke 'I'm fine' Wyatt. "He's not fine! Some idiot hit him."

"Please tell me you didn't hit him back," Gary said, face red and blotchy.

"I can't tell you that, Gary," Luke said, hands in his pockets.

"He had to! The man attacked me." Okay maybe that was an exaggeration, but he'd grabbed her arm, and it had *hurt*.

"Shit! One of Reggie's friends?" Gary said.

Luke turned to Gary. "Some drunk who works the docks,

knew Reggie, and doesn't like the fact that I've got money now. He wanted to take it out on me with his fists."

"Don't worry, the police let Luke go, but took the other guy," Lexi said.

"The *police* were involved?" Gary's hands went to his head.

Lexi worried a fingernail between her teeth. "And some people were...shooting video."

"Dear lord! I'll have to get the fixer on this pronto," Gary said.

"The fixer?" Luke asked. "What the hell is the fixer?"

"D.C., he works for the label and with musicians who get in a little trouble. Any bad press, he makes it go away. He's like that beautiful chick from *Scandal* except that he's a guy."

"Oh, I like that show," Lexi said.

"Guy sounds like a magician," Luke said.

Gary pointed to Luke. "We need to have a talk. A meeting. All hands on deck."

But Luke, not so subtly, grabbed hold of Gary's shoulders and turned him in the direction of the door. "Later."

"This is important. How's it going to look?" Gary stood at the front of the door, hands folded across his chest. "You're going to have a black eye. This is your career we're talking about!"

"This is more important." Luke opened the door for him. He stood there, silently waiting for Gary to take his invitation to leave.

"We'll talk later." Gary went out the door, slamming it in his wake.

"Oh, boy. He looks mad. Ice!" She ran to the kitchen, got a dishtowel, and wrapped ice in it. "It will help with the swelling."

When she got back with the ice, Luke stood in the middle of the living room, staring at her from under hooded lids. "I can't believe—"

"Sit," she ordered, pointing to the couch.

He smirked but obeyed, making a big show of backing up to the couch and sitting down, legs spread open. Such a man. "I said I'm f—"

"Don't!"

If he said the F word one more time, she would flip out. Just do somersaults from the living room to the kitchen, and not in a celebratory way either. She gently pressed the towel to his injured eye.

She'd never had to take care of Luke before. Not like this. He'd always taken care of her. After losing their baby. After The Scandal. After being dumped by the label. He'd always fought for her. On the other hand, she'd been busy defending and fighting for her sister. She'd never had to do much fighting for him. Other than talking her father into letting him roadie for the band, but that hadn't been difficult. Luke had done the rest with his heart and his talent. Daddy had seen something special in Luke and had liked him from day one.

Today, she'd like to think she'd become a bit of a fighter too. In more ways than one.

"You know, if that guy had more of a neck, I might have been able to hang on longer and do some damage," she said.

Luke reached to tuck a stray hair behind her ear. "My little street fighter. I didn't know you had it in you."

She considered it. Only once before had she been so ready to tear someone to pieces, and that had been in front of Lulu's Day Spa last week. Anyone who'd ever tried to hurt her family was fair game. The claws came out.

And now that included Luke. Maybe it always had. "He was trying to hurt you. I would have done anything to stop him."

"Baby, seriously, I appreciate it, but don't ever do that

again." He tipped her palm and brought it up to his lips to kiss it.

"Why?"

He cocked his head like he couldn't believe she'd asked that question. "Guy was three times your size."

"But I shouldn't have had that meltdown. It's just that for a moment I thought maybe...I don't know. I thought even after all your sweet words, you didn't really want *me*. You wanted the song. Another hit. I'm sorry. I somehow got you mixed up with all the men like Gary in Nashville. With all the record label people who take, take, take. But that's never been you."

"Lexi," he said softly, gently, taking her hand. "There are always going to be people around us who mean well. Outsiders. Influencers of every kind in the business. Some will try to come between us. Some of them won't even mean to do it. But if we keep tight with what we have right here, no one can take *this* away from us. Not unless we let them. We have to trust each other because we're all we have. Just us, baby. Just us."

"Luke," she said, because he was drawing her in again. She wanted to believe him.

What had Gary called him? Silver tongued devil. She loved that silver tongue, damn it. Loved it when it pushed past her teeth into her mouth, greedy and hungry. Loved when it was sliding down her body, causing trembles and moans. But there was more. She loved the words he'd said. Words that meant he wanted a life with her at its center, and not *his people* or *her people*. Not music, and not songs. Just the two of them.

For me, you're the song.

This is more important, he'd told Gary.

"You really think so?" she pressed her forehead to his. "We can keep everyone else away?"

"Trust me."

"It's just you and me."

"Forever."

That sounded very familiar, and for the first time in a long while...true.

EPILOGUE

"Always remember that you're unique...just like everyone else." ~ Meme

One month later

The crowd at Tootsie's went nuts as Luke and his band finished *Can't Sleep*. It was his first appearance back in Nashville since his debut album had gone gold, and it felt good to be among old friends and fans. No fan on earth was quite as enthusiastic as a Nashville country music fan. He'd first performed here with the Wilder Sisters years ago, and there were fans here who had been with him that long.

"It's good to be here again," Luke said, taking a seat next to an empty stool with a microphone set-up. "Don't know how many of you know this, but I wrote this next song with my fiancée, Lexi Wilder."

Round of applause and yells from the crowd.

"I see you've heard of her," Luke said, smiling and strumming the opening chords to *Falling for Forever*.

Laughter followed, along with a chorus of "Get her out here," and "Play it!"

"Lexi, baby, would you come out here?"

The crowd went wild when Lexi took her place on the stool next to him, guitar already in hand. She waved and smiled. His heart kicked up a notch because he didn't think he'd ever get used to having her by his side night after night, day after day. He'd once told himself he couldn't be lucky enough to have both the love of his life and his dream career.

Apparently, he'd been wrong.

Luke continued to strum while Lexi got situated at the mike. "Pretty sure you men out there can relate, but I had to beg her to marry me."

Everyone laughed, and Lexi shook her head a couple of times. Rolled her eyes. "Not true."

"I mean, look how beautiful she is."

She leaned into the mike. "Girls, is he gorgeous or what? Would you say no to him?"

This repartee might seem natural, and it was, but also rehearsed ahead of time. Both he and Lexi had agreed to what parts of their private lives they would share. When they'd both returned to Nashville, he'd had a brief meeting with the so-called Fixer. Damien "D.C." Caldwell, a big guy who looked like he'd played pro-football at one time. He'd gone on to explain to both Luke and Lexi that when the press was able to get little pieces of their private lives, they'd be satisfied and less likely to dig for more. Less likely to spread nasty lies and rumors. No guarantees, of course, but it was a good strategy. And so, ahead of time, he and Lexi had decided what they would share about their personal life, and what they would not.

Among the things they would not share was that their wedding would take place back home in Whistle Cove. He'd suggested it, of course, because he knew what would make her happy. It had been decided seconds after he'd asked her to marry him, when she'd phoned her sisters, crying and squealing, telling them that she'd be home for Christmas to plan a wedding.

They had only been back in Nashville two weeks when he'd asked her to marry him. He'd picked out the ring ahead of time, a huge solitaire rock that cost the same as the tricked out 4 wheel drive truck he'd been eying. Waited for the right time. Their routine had been that each day they would head to the studio and each afternoon shop for a house on the outskirts of Nashville. One look at the sprawling ranch style mansion with a wrap-around porch, horse stables, and most importantly, a huge dining room, and Lexi declared the house to be *the one*. She planned on hosting many family holiday gatherings.

He hadn't wanted to wait another minute, so right after he'd agreed the house was the one, he'd gone on bended knee in the marbled foyer. She'd said yes, and that was it for him. His one and only. Forever. He'd never be happier in his life.

Now he'd be a husband and a homeowner.

A long way from the docks and a life as the son of Reggie Wyatt. He'd finally found his way in the world. Finally chased all the demons away. He knew he deserved this now. Deserved her. Since she told him how much she loved him over and over every night in bed, he was going to go ahead and believe it. Believe her.

Lexi played the intro to *Falling for Forever*, and glanced at him with a smile full of heart. Waiting.

He started singing, knowing she'd join him in the chorus.

The End
And also the beginning...

If you've enjoyed this novel, please sign up for Heatherly's newsletter. You will receive two free novellas. Keep up to date with flash sales, future releases, and all the fun stuff, like naming secondary characters and pets.
Coming on November 9, 2018
SHE'S COUNTRY STRONG,
A Wilder Sisters novel

ALSO BY HEATHERLY BELL:

All of Me

Somebody like You

Until there was You

Anywhere with You, a novella

Unforgettable You

Forever with You

Crazy for You: Christmas in Starlight Hill

Only You, a novella (coming soon)

Heroes of Fortune Valley series with Harlequin Superromance:

Breaking Emily's Rules

Airman to the Rescue

This Baby Business

The Right Man, a novella

Coming in July of 2019 from Harlequin Special Edition:

Wildfire Ridge

ABOUT THE AUTHOR

Heatherly Bell is the author of fifteen contemporary romances. She drinks too much coffee, craves cupcakes, and occasionally wears real pants. She lives in northern California with her family.

You can find her all over social media, posting about her dogs, and the eternal battle over carbs.

Heatherly@HeatherlyBell.com
www.HeatherlyBell.com